# PANEGYRIC

# PANEGYRIC

*A Novel*

# LOGAN MACNAIR

| N₁ | O₂ | N₁ |

**CANADA**

*Publisher's note: This book is a work of fiction. Names, characters, places and
incidents are either the product of the author's imagination or are used
fictitiously, and any resemblance to actual persons living or dead
is entirely coincidental.*

**Library and Archives Canada Cataloguing in Publication**

Title: Panegyric : a novel / Logan Macnair.

Names: Macnair, Logan, 1989– author.

Identifiers: Canadiana 20200168568 | ISBN 9781988098975 (softcover)

Classification: LCC PS8625.N335 P36 2020 | DDC C813/.6—dc23

Printed and bound in Canada on 100% recycled paper.

**Now Or Never Publishing**
901, 163 Street
Surrey, British Columbia
Canada V4A 9T8

**nonpublishing.com**
*Fighting Words.*

We gratefully acknowledge the support of the Canada Council for the Arts
and the British Columbia Arts Council for our publishing program.

*To Ashley,*

*For nudging me off the diving board*
*and into the unexpectedly calm waters beneath.*

*But the skylight is like skin for a drum I'll never mend,*
*and all the rain falls down amen,*
*on the works of last year's man.*
                    —Leonard Cohen, *Last Year's Man*

I

# PROLEGOMENON

"Do you know who I am?"

Do I know who you are? Aren't you the cynosure we were all meant to emulate? Aren't you the heartbeat of industry recently recalibrated to match the rhythm of modern apogee? Are you the towering presence that thought to strike out with such a piercing and focused query or are you the resonant timbre with which it was released? Anyone with even the slightest read on Canada's political pulse would know who you are. But do I know who you are? Based on common titles I do. Member of Parliament. Self-made millionaire. Prodigious businessman turned equally successful politician. Likely future leader of the federal party and possibly the nation. These were things I knew, but there were also things I had heard. Direct. Strong. Intense. Dangerous. A marriage of such adjectives and a moment to thank those timid enough to refuse having their hearts painted over by the same brush. These things I did not mention. And then his question:

"Do you know who I am?"

I was busy figuring out who I was at the time. I knew what they said about me. They said I lack form and discipline, that I am allergic to plot and structure, choked purple in the face, that nothing I write will ever see the light of day lest I learn to play by the rules. But somehow he knew who I was, even when nobody was supposed to. He knew that I had recently ghostwritten the memoirs of a former premier, even when my name was refused space on the cover. He knew exactly where and when he would be able to find me to ask this question:

"Do you know who I am?"

And that was the question that brought me some 4000 kilometers across the nation from the mattress in the corner of my Vancouver apartment to the basement office of his Oshawa home, sandwiched between an opulent suburb and a private entry into the waters of Lake Ontario. His proposition was a simple one—'tell them who I am, in my own words.' He spoke of lavish payment, of idyllic living conditions, of the freedom to work my own hours so long as I could finish the project by the end of the summer. And so here I am, settling in to what will be my home for the next five months and the task at hand. I've been here nearly a week, yet I still can't shake the question that started it all:

"Do you know who I am?"

Aren't you Maxime Montblanc, born 1959 in British Columbia's sleepy interior to Québécois parents newly relocated? Surely you are the success story that we were all meant to be. But are you truly Canada's brightest light? Are you the embodiment of resilience yet to become inured by the dancing pistons of modern machinery? Are you the pleasant, well-mannered man that solicited my services? Are you the ruthless and perfidious harbinger of ruination they say you are?

I thought I knew who Maxime Montblanc was at the time. As it turns out, I had no idea. But I learned. And you will too.

## 2

# PROLIXITY

ORWELL INSTRUCTED WRITERS of all vocations to avoid using long words when there was a short one that might suitably replace it. Hemingway echoed this notion, arguing that big emotions don't necessarily come from big words.

As an infant I had a precocious disposition toward reading that my parents proudly encouraged by surrounding me with books. By the age of five I was reading beyond the expected level, though my pronunciation was marked with a noticeable stutter and I had trouble forming full sentences without tripping over certain words. My parents and their friends thought this was cute at the time. By the age of ten my stutter had become significantly worse to the point where nearly every word was a struggle. As teachers started questioning my intelligence, as other kids started their imitations and mockery, and as I grew increasingly quiet and afraid to speak, it wasn't so cute anymore. And now at thirty years old, though my stutter is as pronounced and debilitating as ever, I've had my whole life to deal with this master status the best I can and to accept certain things that at this point cannot be changed. I know I won't be starting any conversations with any alluring strangers I see in public. I know I'll never be a contestant on *Jeopardy!* I know I'll never deliver any keynotes, best-man speeches, lectures, or eulogies. And I know that to compensate for this I will always disregard the advice of Orwell and Hemingway.

Maxime Montblanc personally recruited me to ghostwrite his memoirs because he had heard that I was capable of completing this task with the same quality that he demonstrates in all other aspects of his life, but between you and me, I think he may have been misinformed. Regardless, he was unaware of my condition at the time he solicited my services but he has so far demonstrated a high degree of patience and empathy. Most people do. I've had a long time to acclimate to the lexicon of pity that I am routinely exposed to. Still, in the week that I have been living in the basement guestroom of Monty's Oshawa home he has proven to be a courteous and respectful host. Under such conditions, spending the entirety of the emerging summer here to write his memoirs sure beats the hell out of spending another summer languishing amid the rolling waves of underachievement.

But as I soon learned, my arrangement with Mister Maxime Montblanc—the highly esteemed paragon of politics—was to be far more multifarious than the simple writing of a book.

# 3

## PROMULGATION

"IT IS TIME that we discussed your impediment."

"What imp-p-p-imp–imped–imp–impediment?"

"Clever boy. Funny boy. Still, I would rather not do you the discourtesy of pretending that your problem is invisible. I would prefer that we be transparent about it, for this arrangement will only succeed if we remain fluid in all things. We must appear as translucent to one another. I need you to see me unfiltered and without pretense or expectation. If I am to trust you with writing the story of my life, I must also be assured that you see me complete. This is a trust that must be reciprocally felt. No hollow peaks tickling the azure and no rolling sediment. A subject within and a magnified gaze inverted inward. A man uses a chainsaw to fell a tree, but what fool of a man would not first familiarize himself with the innards and mechanics of the tool itself? Do you understand?"

"Yes."

"Good. Good boy. A good boy, and one able-bodied enough and undeniably of sound mind. I see in your words an intellect that hovers above the vacant stares of the crowded congregation below. You are a rightful heir of appreciation, but am I correct to assume that not many acknowledge your birthright? Your teachers and classmates, they all thought you were retarded, didn't they?"

"Suh-suh-sssome of them d-d-did."

"Yes, of course they did. But that is far from the truth, isn't it? There is no established link between intelligence and those who stutter, is there?"

"No."

"No, there isn't. Of course you would know that. Though I suspect that little piece of information failed to console you as a child. I don't imagine that made the taunting hurt any less. No, it didn't make you feel any better about yourself at all, did it?"

"Na-na-not really, no."

"I can feel your hesitation, Lawrence. I know these are tumultuous waters that you are not particularly eager to navigate, but I will thank you for your continued endurance and bravery. What you have endured will surely not be undone by my continued probing. Now then, modern science has yet to pinpoint a specific cause for stuttering, correct?"

"Yes."

"Nor has there been any consensus on a cure?"

"No, b-b-b-but there are tuh-treatments and, and, and, and therapies."

"And you have attempted them all, haven't you?"

"Yes."

"And yet you stand before me with what is undoubtedly the worst speech impediment I have ever personally witnessed. The treatments did not work for you, did they?"

"No."

"No, they certainly did not. And yet you have made habits of some of the practices, haven't you? You still speak very slowly, you still change certain words that you know will be troublesome, you still take deep breaths from the diaphragm and over-enunciate, don't you?"

"Yes."

"And you're still afraid to be introduced to new people, aren't you?"

"Yes."

"You're terrified of asking a stranger for the time or for directions, aren't you?"

"Yes."

"You dread having to place your order at a restaurant, don't you?"

"Yes."

"Because people still think that you are retarded when they hear you speak, don't they?"

"Yes."

"And so you've immersed yourself in the written language. You have overcompensated for your inability to communicate verbally by learning how to communicate through the magic of the written word, haven't you?"

"Yes."

"Something tells me that you have studied the dictionary in some detail. Am I correct?"

". . . Yes."

"All of those complex and complicated words, all of those beautiful and obscure words that are seldom seen in common conversation, all of those lovely words that lend themselves so well to poetry and prose, all of those words that you would never be able to properly say. I've noticed it's the 'P' words that you have the most trouble with, isn't?"

"Yes."

"I imagine that engaging in romantic endeavors must be quite the ordeal for you."

"It can be."

"It is, you darling boy, it surely is. And here you are, thirty years old and unmarried. As I understand it, the prognosis for adults is not promising. You will likely have this debilitating condition for the remainder of your life. You may be able to mask it at times, but surely you must have accepted now that this is and forever will be a part of you?"

"Yes."

"You cannot speak French, can you?"

"No."

"Oh, you wonderful boy, of course not. Have you ever imagined your wedding day? Have you felt the terror creep up the hairs of your arm when you picture a man of God speaking to you those inevitable and sacred words? 'Do you, Lawrence, take this woman, to have and to told, in sickness and in health, until death do you part?' Have you practiced your response?"

"No."

"Very good. But surely you must feel as if time is running out for you?"

"Uh-al-almmmost."

"Brilliant. Brilliant young man. You've the soul of a cosmopolitan with wings tragically clipped. So true a form that I can feel myself weep. There is not another person on this planet who I would have tell the story of my life. This world is too much. No, it's not enough. *Non terminus.* I have tested the limits of my empathy, endeavored to feel the phantom pain of amputated limbs, the loss of a mother tongue, but I am at once negligent and diminutive to your plight. I have become a champion of the market, a leader of the nation, and a master of myself all because of my ability to say exactly what needed to be said in any given situation. I have made my millions and repeatedly earned my Parliamentary seat from an impeccable insight into the social condition, yes, but all of this would be wasted without a vessel from which to strike. You beautiful boy. I will never know the angels in your privileged vision, but pray that I might one day find the talent to translate a sorrow as sweet as yours. Look at me, Larry. See through me as I am starting to see through you. Do not leave me wandering alone and unrequited. Fly beside me with your broken wings and we may yet reach the teasing shores of placidity."

# 4

## POETASTERS

AND DEATH TO the Hacks!

I see them gnashing away at levity as they do, sucking on life's rind with their uncut teeth. Proper indications of fatalism with their 'born to be' discourse, each of them anomalously persuaded that they are painting with the inherited brush of Picasso. I see them walking the hippest streets of Montreal and Vancouver, eyes toward the sky and shouting at the unresponsive ether for a sign of validation. They step on my toes as they pass, ignoring me and my bad haircut. And what are they to offer but another muzzled voice?

And disdain for the Hacks!

And their cleverness, quantifiable as currency, and their words, intriguingly arranged, but predictable as ever. I know their warped vision. They view each of their outputs as rungs on a ladder. Callous calculations spinning in their thoughts, they would eat the heart of you or I so long as an audience would be formed. And what of their gift, absorbed through the blood of Apollo, that courses through their veins? No, you members of the inane gaggle, a gift not conducive to condemnation is no gift at all.

And examination of the Hacks!

Who once upon a time discovered the sway that they held over the bisexual nymphets, moon-grass grazers, and precarious exhibitionists who so keenly took to the untouchable mediums of this new century. And let this further illuminate the distinctions between us. Know that I would willingly castrate myself if it meant that I could work more peacefully. And while their cocks were being massaged to whispers of suicide pacts and elopement, I would sit unaccompanied under dim light with a growing collection of unread postulations, the existence of which I could never be fully sure of. A tree falls in a forest, but that doesn't get anybody laid.

And empathy for the Hacks!

Because we are one and the same. Astute readers would have already picked up on that. You are safe and you are correct to judge me. The arrows I volley are not shot from a bow of otherworldly material, nor are they readied by untarnished hands. My first taste of tangible success came fairly recently with the publication of *Restoring Conviction: The Hope and Faith of a Public Servant,* and while my name was not allowed anywhere near it, I read every single review and followed the public and critical reaction to that book like a man possessed. Are these the actions of an enlightened creator? No, these are the actions of a eunuch who has retained a trace of feeling in his groin. These are the actions of a Hack.

And envy for the Hacks . . .

Because I know the things I would do to be openly counted amongst their ranks. Because I've often dreamed up a life where I am not just accepted by them, but embraced. I want to walk their streets with shoes unscuffed. I want to be their chosen king, the man who came from nothing, the man whose bad haircut they all now emulate. I want the keys to their Royal Palace and the secret backroom where the elite congregate and hand jobs are wordlessly initiated.

And now a parting gift for the Hacks.

This is tearing me up. Quartered by my arms and their genuine desire to gesture something that matters and my legs and their commitment to standing tall on the cliffs of contrarianism. I was once told never to offer advice to those who do not ask for it. I adhere to this, though ironically, I didn't ask for that particular piece of advice when it was given to me. So if these words are to be immediately dissipated and lost to the wind before reaching unwelcoming ears, this I will accept.

Ready then?

Neverkisssanguinelipsneverguideinlawlessshipsneverwatchrustbeformedneverdanceintorridstormsneverdrinkfromunknownuttersneverliewithtwooldloversneverbreakwithscriptedwavesneverdelveinunclaimedcavesneverbuildwithflawlessnailsneverrepeatoncetoldtalesneversignwithborrowedpensneverboundtowardeasyendsneverpraytofadingflamesnevergorgeonfetteredfamenevercalltheclearestbluffsandneversleeponjustenough.

# 5

## PROCRASTINATION

RECALL, IF YOU will, the modern fable of the man with no mirror in his bathroom. He styled his hair by watching his shadow on the wall. Now squeeze from this tale a moral that I might use to anchor this bloody chapter that I've been stuck on all day. I've settled quite quietly into a new routine under the divine protection of my new landlord. Yes, he my trusted innkeeper, my personal concierge, dutifully assuring that all my earthly needs are continually met. And what have I to offer in return? An empty page, willfully defiant. I haven't been outside today. Come to think of it, I haven't been outside all week. I don't need that kind of unpredictability. No, I'll stick to the formula. 'Keep playing my game,' as the professional athletes say. Do we need to keep this grounded? Forget it. I'm all for demystification these days. Peel off the veneer, see how the sausage is made, anything to compromise the charade. It looks like this:

7:30 am—Wake up to the same family of birds singing their ancestral aria on repeat. A two-note tune, once pleasant, though more resemblant of an atonal factory whistle of late. The sheets of Montblanc's guestroom bed absorb me.

8:00 am—Breakfast with Montblanc. We go over the day's plan, he tells me stories, he moralizes and philosophizes, he helps me find the character. 'Don't put that part in the book', he'll tell me. I take notes. I tune in and out. He leaves to go shake hands and kiss babies and take his place in the grand assembly line of progress and leadership. What a model of a man. I'm so blessed and humbled to be in a situation where I can learn from him and . . . oh, he's gone? Good, time to get to it.

9:00 am—The work day begins. I dig through boxes of documents both political and personal to get a sense of my subject. Meeting schedules, voting records, personal justifications for the nation-shaping decisions he helped make, a journal entry detailing his trip to the Party's national convention in Edmonton, who he had dinner with, the son-of-a-bitch who wasn't going to last, the quality of the towels at the hotel, the name of the escort, the colour of her underwear, it's all a rich tapestry you see. It's a jigsaw puzzle with no edge pieces. My grandma taught me to start with the edge pieces. Lot of good that's doing now. These documents allow me to sketch out a black and white picture, Montblanc's explanations fill it with colour, and lo, the template for a soon-to-be bestselling memoir dances like Persephone incarnate.

11:30 pm—A light lunch. I recall one of the rules laid down by my hospitable host, 'help yourself to any food you like.' The overabundance of choice and the inherent perils it provides. Our modern dilemma. When you can do anything you end up doing nothing. The emptiest of feelings crawling up my legs. Inevitably I just make a turkey sandwich and shut up about it.

12:00 pm—Begin writing. Compile all the elements and paint them onto the page. Remember to say it in his voice, but don't use too many big words—it turns off casual readers. This needs to be accessible, not elitist. Keep it just sophisticated enough so that anyone can read it while ensuring that those who do will feel smart and informed. Something you can be proud to have on your bookshelf. Obsessively check dates and facts to make sure no mistakes are being made. Produce something that I can proudly show to Monty. Question why his approval is so important to me. Assure myself that I don't have to do any of this, that I'm free to leave whenever I want. Remember how much money I'm being paid to do this. Realize that for the right price there's probably nothing that I wouldn't do. Call myself pathetic, but then remember that this is indicative of the society we live in and the importance that it places on financial accumulation, and not on my own materialistic greed. Feel slightly better, though self-aware enough to accept that I can only hide behind my shallow rationalizations for increasingly limited periods of time. To research and write an entire book over the course of just a few months requires a substantial daily output. I heard that Stephen King writes 2000 words per diem. I put my ambition on trial.

6:00 pm—Stop writing. It's quittin' time. I don't care if I'm on a roll. My ambition pleads not guilty.

7:00 pm—Dinner. Sometimes with M, sometimes alone. Depends on whether or not he's out of town, and more importantly, whether or not he wants to see me. When we do meet it gives me a chance to show him what I have completed. When he doesn't like it, I make mental notes for revision. When he does, I allow myself a quick moment of internal validation. Gentle dinner conversation usually follows. At the end of the day I find him more prone toward waxing lyrically—at times in a manner annoyingly opaque. I know him as a man that enjoys having an audience, even if I am the sole member. I try to just listen, though buried in his voluble soliloquies are occasional moments that arouse a curiosity in me. Some nights I ask and some nights he is jovial and eager enough to engage in mutually enjoyable discussion. Some nights he verbally berates me. Some nights we sit in total silence. I suspect his sex life must resemble these dynamics.

9:00 pm—M retires to his bedroom on the top floor. I don't know what he does up there. As per one of the other established rules of my tenure I am never to venture to the top floor. I return to the guestroom in the basement. If I am feeling ambitious I might make some edits on the day's writing. I never feel ambitious.

★★★

And such is the clockwork of my current existence. It is currently 3:39 pm and I've yet to produce anything substantial. Anything at all if we're being completely transparent about it. Lack of material maybe? I find myself struggling with the overwhelming desire to go to the bathroom and smash the mirror, though I relent, and opt instead to stare at the blank screen in front of me for the next two hours and twenty-one minutes.

# 6

## PROTHALAMION

I KNEW BIG M was married and I had seen him and his wife on TV once before. She was delivering a speech on behalf of some environmental group whose name I can't recall, urging politicians to do more in the fight against climate change. I remember the fervor of her environmentalism juxtaposed against the steamrolling industry spearheaded by her dear husband. Despite this, I saw her the way that I assume many others did, as an inherently likable person. Attractive, articulate, compassionate, and with an impeccable sense of style. I had expected to meet her upon arriving at Château Montblanc, but nearly two weeks had passed since beginning my residence and she had yet to be seen. Her prolonged absence was curious to me and so at dinner tonight I decided to ask M where his wife was.

"Wuh-wuh-wuh-where your wife was?"

"I beg your pardon?"

"I meant wuh-where is your wuh-wife?"

"Out of town."

Brevity and hesitation! The plot thickens. Usually Max's responses to my questions were prolonged to the point that I regret asking them in the first place. Something's afoul here. Better do a little sleuthing to get to the bottom of this.

"For wuh-wuh-wuh-work?"

"Work? Her job is being my wife."

His front isn't budging. Let me try once more.

"Is she c-c-c-coming huh-huh-home sssss-suh-soon?"

"You will never meet her, Lawrence. Do not forget what you are here to do."

It's hard to get a read on what's happening right now. Is he being overprotective of her? He never struck me as that insecure. I nod in the affirmative and we wait in silence for a moment before he makes an unexpected but welcome proposition.

"Very well . . . You truly wish to know where she is now?"

I nod in the affirmative.

"Indeed then, but I will caution you not to interrupt me whilst I'm speaking. Can you assure me of this?"

I nod in the affirmative and Monty begins filling me in on the current state of his marital circumstances.

"Twenty-two years ago it was 'dearly beloved' and my forehead sweating under the stage lights as I ticked away the seconds until the next act break. Today, she lives in my home, but no longer in my heart. Ours is no longer a union made under God and witnessed by the State, no, we are today bigger strangers than we have ever been before. This was not amongst the images cutting through my mind when I took a knee before her to declare in sincerity our future. She dwells in these walls as a breathing body with oxygen unshared. Gradual was the displacement, and where is she now? Out west, visiting her sister, visiting her mother, visiting ex-lovers that are providing the amorous attention that I no longer can. And when shall she return? Assuredly in time for the election campaign's commencement, as punctual as ever. And she will kiss me as I take the stage, the lips once welcoming, later poisonous, presently a prop. She will applaud me with a calming smile affixed to her face as I profess my love and gratitude to her from center stage. And so perfectly cast is our charade. Myself, the soon leader of this nation, and my brilliant wife, strong yet nurturing, fashionable yet not materialistic or shallow. The boxes have been checked and the team is convinced that she appeals to most demographics. A flawlessly concocted blend, an old-fashioned soul with modern sensibilities, well tapped-in to the cultural milieu. And how natural she looks in the photos she takes with the dullards of the upper echelon. She speaks confidently though not haughtily or condescendingly when she makes the case for increased environmental protection and the importance of education. Yes, indeed, our children are the most valuable resource we have. And after the performance we return to the hollowed hallowed halls of our home. Our master bedroom, a former Pangea, now islands gradually drifting from their origin point. And witness the contents of my heart, extracted and exhausted. There is no contempt anymore. There is no hate or disdain. Worse—there is nothing. No spectrum of emotion to enliven our condition, no influence of unpredictability, just an empty space between us and within us. No contact, no wasted words, and none of the conversational dancing that brought us to that moment twenty-two years ago with the 'dearly beloved' and my forehead sweating under the stage lights. No, this is our existence now. An eternal ruse, mutually beneficial and without the fear of irrationality. We glide safely into the waters of stoicism, not in love, not in danger. And when the light of lecherous thoughts shine through into vision, I reflect them onto the bodies of new strangers and old familiars. I once concealed any evidence of my lascivious liaisons out of respect, but that courtesy has evaporated, and with it, any attempts of subtlety. The whores come to my home directly now and we play in the guest bedroom while my wife sleeps a staircase apart. She pays no mind so long as we keep our decibels in check.

"If I am elected Prime Minister we shall continue this farce. She will play her part as expertly as I have come to expect. If I am not then we will have no reason to remain in each other's lives and that will be that. Ours is now a marriage of convenience, bereft of the love that we once vowed to always maintain. Do you understand?"

Eye gnawed indie afore motive.

"I no longer have any endearing words to say about her. But as your perceptive mind might have already guessed, that will be your part to play. You will be responsible for writing our story in the words that I have forgotten to speak. But that will come in due time. For now, I will ask your permission to leave this topic of conversation behind. Is that agreeable with you?"

I nod in the affirmative (and those words officially lose all meaning to me). I take a moment to reflect on what Max had just told me and decide to redefine my parameters of lost meaning.

## 7

## POSTERITY

LEGACY, DICTATOR OF my calendar, bedfellow of my purpose. My deficit, my debt. Leg-ah-see: the tip of the tongue taking a trip—actually, hold on, best to stop there if I intend to keep my letter-box free from sternly-worded warnings from folks representing the estate of Nabokov. Leg. Ah. See. And let that then be the word of the day, however you choose to internalize it.

Enter Cornelius Nepos, a name with which you are likely unfamiliar (and rightly so). What was his connection to Cicero, a name with which you are likely familiar (and rightly so)? The majority of the works written by Nepos were unfortunately lost to the sea of time, so what legacy of him remains? I will pray at your altar Nepos. I will have your name seen in print once again. You, my unadorned ancestor of the backstage, shall find life anew in the fickle netting of my own legacy. Life like a flicker, while my heart is lit aflame like a Viking funeral. And if my bloodline can be traced back to Nepos, then Montblanc's could certainly be traced back to Cicero. And I can't make it any clearer for you beyond that I'm afraid.

Legacy. Again, let the word percolate through the soils of memory until you have arrived at a refined definition. Can the legacy of one be assigned an arbitrary value to be directly compared to that of another? Operationalize and quantify the concept. Is it the stinging sensation in the genitals after copulation? A promise in nine months delivered? Tread on the dirty bills, I always walk barefoot in the summer, it hurts at first but the soles don't take long to toughen up. Funny how far our luxuries remove us from the legacies of the past. Maybe it's a direct articulation of name noto-riety. By the time this is all over, every national newspaper in the country is sure to make mention of Montblanc at least once in every issue. You won't find my name anywhere within those pages, however, if you are taking the trip from mainland B.C. to Vancouver Island and happen to be aboard the ferry, '*Spirit of British Columbia*', you will find, in the video-arcade area located on the starboard side of the vessel, a *Donkey Kong* cabinet. Focus on the screen of this cabinet and eventually the high scores will be displayed. At the top of this list of high scores, and by quite a safe margin if I may be afforded a small boast, you will find the triad of letters 'LSM'. My initials. My legacy.

Then again, I've never been one to question the will of the seraphim. Lower your head in respect, count on your right hand the blessings.

On my thumb, showing to myself an early sign of approval, I count the gifts left by Johann Strauss II. My body never could answer the call to coordination, barring me from all but the blurriest of dance floors, but imagination affords us the opportunity to see ourselves move in wondrous projections. I am waltzing in perfect synergy with my partner as the eyes of the room follow us in hypnotic admiration. I am, therefore, I think.

On my index, my hand now making the shape of an L and signifying to myself the 'loser' gesture, I will count as one collective some of my missing memories. I don't remember the sands of Juno beach shifting under my boots—vacate my legacy. Nor do I remember loving hands being laid upon me in any fashion that might betray the authenticity of that adjective. I don't remember water filling my lungs or the aftermath of cracking leather upon my back.

On my middle digit, occasionally called upon to be raised in isolation against those who would insult the honour of its host, I count the open doors lining the horizon. Let it be known that the absence of legacy is not entirely without reward.

On my ring finger, ever naked as its adjacent brother, I count the plentiful salmon of British Columbia, caught, cured, smoked, and served to me amidst the company of those dearest and closest to branch. Affirm joy in the most base of needs and pray that they remain forever met.

On my pinky, once used to bind the most solemn of my youthful oaths, I count the quarter in my pocket that allowed me the opportunity to climb to the top of the *Donkey Kong* scoreboard and assert my legacy. It may be a beggarly legacy of velleity, but it belongs to me, untarnished and perhaps not respectable, but admissible. And maybe that's enough.

That was a reassuring exercise. I don't think I could be bothered to do it every day though. Not enough room in the morning routine. Maybe the life of Cornelius Nepos isn't any of my concern. Maybe I'll go to Hawaii for my honeymoon and meet another couple while I'm there. We will drink and laugh and then part ways and never see each other again. And that will be the only trace that the legacy of Mr. and Mrs. So-and-So will ever leave on me. Will they lie awake at night pondering that doom? Doubtful I imagine. There's a lesson to be learned there I suppose.

Fine. I admit obscurity. That's right children. Raid your piggy banks. Search the cushions of your couches. Sell watered-down lemonade. Pester your parents. Do whatever you can to collect as many quarters as possible. Take them to video-arcade area located on the starboard side of the *Spirit of British Columbia*. Keep pumping them into that *Donkey Kong* cabinet. Beat my high score. Shatter it! Play as if your future depended on it . . .

One day your legacy might.

# 8

## Parallelisms

IT's BEEN A month since I've come under the secret employ of Mister Maxime the Marvelous and I've settled nicely into a stable routine of sorts. I do research, I learn things about MMM, some uninspired words get written, I struggle with what the critics would refer to as my 'selling out', I remind myself that I don't have any critics. Lather. Rinse. Repeat. That said, while this has thus far been a strange and wondrous world to inhabit, I do often find myself pining for the simpler life I lead back home in British Columbia. I'm not sure why that is, Montblanc's house is a palace, better in every conceivable way than that crap-shack of an apartment I call home. Well, on second thought, I do know why. But it's only when the two domiciles are directly compared that this becomes clear.

★★★

*Apartment 315*—Home. Located in plain sight somewhere in the dodgy outskirts of Vancouver. There's a stained mattress in the corner of my bedroom, still made up and waiting for me to return.

*Château Montblanc*—What is currently home. Located in partial isolation somewhere in an affluent residential section of Oshawa. There's a queen-sized bed in the basement guestroom that I have no idea how to properly make.

*Apartment 315*—It never stops raining. The locals still find unique ways to comment on this, though most of them have accepted it as a way of life and act as if the shitty weather has some baptismal power that inundates them into the divine protection of their metropolitan overlord. The courtyard of my apartment resembles an impassable marsh for most of the year. Even on atypical days of dryness, you can't walk across it without your feet sinking into the water inconspicuously collected under the surface. I can look out my third-floor window and see the reservoir of rainwater slowly expand and turn opaque as it absorbs the surrounding filth of the unkempt courtyard.

*Château Montblanc*—I can look out M's dining room window and see the faintly rippling cerulean water of Lake Ontario. The warmth of the Oshawa summer has compelled me into that lake a few times now, and while I'm not much of a swimmer, the crispness of the water has proven its invigorative properties. The grass leading from M's back door to the lake is characteristically manicured and visibly lush. I don't think it has rained once since I've arrived here. I'm not sure if that's normal and I have no desire to ask any of the locals if it is. There's a consistent redolence in the air that remains uncompromised by the industries of Toronto some sixty kilometers to the west.

*Apartment 315*—The hallway of my building reeks of secondhand smoke and wet dog despite the fact that neither smoking nor dogs are allowed inside. Today is Sunday. Normally at this time I would be carrying my cracked plastic laundry basket through this malodorous hallway and down the uncarpeted steps to the shared laundry room on the bottom level. Two coin-operated washing machines and two coin-operated drying machines for the entire building to share. Sundays are particularly bad since it's the preferred laundry day of many of the residents, but if I can get down there early enough I can usually avoid the congestion. The laundry room is claustrophobic and derelict. Beside the sink are some crusted magazines that have been there since I moved in. I swear someone is stealing my socks one at a time and I shudder to think as to what their reasons for doing so might be.

*Château Montblanc*—The laundry room in M's house is bigger than my bedroom back home. The interface on his machines resemble an airplane cockpit and I'm too embarrassed to ask for help. I can do laundry here whenever I want. No wait and no stolen socks. Though the laundry room is just down the hall from the office where I work, the machines run with the type of silence that parliamentarian money can easily afford.

*Apartment 315*—The guy in the unit beneath me keeps the volume on when he watches porn. We both prefer to keep our bedroom windows open, though the price that I pay to take in a little fresh air are the snippets of skin-slapping smut sounds that occasionally waft up. I've met him a couple of times, he can't be more than nineteen or twenty. Living away from home for the first time I imagine and still getting used to the freedoms his new life affords. He's a nice kid, if only lacking in situational and spatial awareness. When it's not the aural waves of what sounds like very conventional porn rising up into my room, it's the marijuana smoke he blows out his window after inhaling from his unnecessarily large bong that I'm sure he's very proud to show off to his friends. It doesn't really bother me. In fact, I see him as something of a kindred spirit. The world turns and the guy downstairs smokes pot, jerks off, and eats microwaveable food. I'm not much of a cook myself.

*Château Montblanc*—Max is a terrific chef—because of course he is—and his kitchen is full of ingredients, appliances, and utensils that I wouldn't know how to use even if I wanted to. In his absence I mainly stick to making sandwiches, albeit with slightly more expensive condiments than I'm used to. Taking a cue from the oblivious second-story stoner back home, I make a continual effort to be a respectful and cleanly guest. Big M isn't going to hear the salacious sounds of filthy films coming from my room. As a matter of fact, I've been ignoring any lecherous desires whatsoever since I've arrived. But I'll be damned if it's not getting harder. Innuendo not intended. The mind wanders. I believe M's closest neighbours are another rich, white couple. I've seen them outside once or twice. I think the wife might be quite attractive for an older lady but I haven't been able to catch a proper glimpse.

*Apartment 315*—There's a cute, purple-haired girl that lives on the other side of the building, though I wonder, is her perceived cuteness one of those 'thirsty in the desert' situations? That's a terrible thing to say, no wonder she hasn't invited me over yet. If I look out my bedroom window I can just barely see into her kitchen, which I promise is not something that I do regularly. Sometimes she's washing dishes at the sink and I find myself encumbered with questions. What does the rest of her apartment look like? The layout is surely the same as mine, but how has she arranged it? What does her bedroom look like? What does she keep in the drawer beside her bed? What might I find in the boxes at the bottom of her closet? This line of questioning carries on for some time and soon I'm thinking of potential names for our children. Yeah, better tap the brakes on that for now. My periwinkle-peaked peer across the building is but one contributor to the larger collective I find myself entangled in. Even though I don't really know any of my neighbours, it's still comforting to belong to a community—except when it isn't. Which is often. I get woken up both late and early to the surrounding cacophony of merriment and argument. Here's some free counselling to the couple above me—if you fight so much, why not just break up? When it's not the louts in immediate earshot it's the constant traffic or the construction across the road. There's always noise, but if it gets any louder I might just snap.

*Château Montblanc*—If it gets any quieter I might just snap. There's still consistent sound to be sure, but it's not the artificial, gauge-reddening noise found back home, it's *sound*. It's birds and insects, and once the faint horns of *Amazing Grace* rising from the horizon, though I may have just imagined that. With no jarring audible distractions I am free to focus on my work undisturbed. Yup. Just me and my work. Just me sitting in a naturally-lit office surrounded by the soothing sounds of serenity. Just me and a pile off stuff to do and nothing in the way to stop me. I wonder what that couple back home is fighting about right now. I'm going to be so far behind on their saga when I finally get back. Oh, and would you look at this? A mostly yellow butterfly is loitering in the air just beyond the window. What's up, pal? You want to kick it with me for a bit? Nope, she's gone. Seems that even the insects here tend to be goal-oriented.

*Apartment 315*—There's a spider that lives just outside my bedroom window. I've named her Wolfish. She's made herself quite the prosperous life too, her web always seems to have company. In my more macabre moments I've spent long stretches watching her interact with her prey. I think it's hypnotic, but maybe I'm just lazy. When the rain and winds come more violently than usual I see her web thrash back and forth and I wonder if it will still be there the next morning. It always is. She's getting fatter too. Is it because of her prowess as a huntress or did some suave man-spider melt the ice around her heart? I never said goodbye to Wolfish before I left, but I feel that she will still be there when I return, stalwart as ever. Someone really ought to talk to the landlord about the pest problem in the building though. I try to avoid him whenever possible, fly under the radar and all that. He's a stern man, Romanian, I think. Never seen him smile. I haven't had any problems with him myself but I have heard other tenants complaining about him.

*Château Montblanc*—Of course I've heard lots of people complain about my current landlord at *Château Montblanc* as well. They say that he's going to steer the nation in the wrong direction, that he's going to run it like a business, not like a country, that he's going to forget about the people who are struggling. When I am surrounded by reminders of his achievements as I am now it becomes easy to forget that Montblanc is quite a divisive figure, even within his own party. There are a lot of people out there who are going to do everything in their power to ensure that M doesn't gain any more influence. I suppose my job is to do the opposite.

*Apartment 315*—And that's the type of reasoning that leads my mind back home. To that place I wanted to leave but couldn't. But I could live in hope with something to work for. Wretches unbound by paved roads saddled with those of us who would count the potholes we cross.

*Château Montblanc*—And that's the type of reasoning that opens my eyes to where I am now. To that place I can leave any time but don't want to. I stand at the top of expectation peering over the edge and suddenly I can't find within myself the constitution required to take another step forward.

# 9

## PENITENCE

THE RIGHT HONOURABLE Kim Campbell is unique amongst the register of former Canadian Prime Ministers for one very important reason. Know what it is?

At forty-six years old she was comparatively young when she first took the office, but no, she wasn't the youngest. That distinction belongs to Joe Clark, who was only thirty-nine when he was first elected to the position.

Campbell's tenure as Prime Minister lasted a paltry 132 days, and while this is indeed significantly shorter than the average, it is not the shortest. That record belongs to Charles Tupper's sixty-eight-day term. Unlikely a coincidence, Tupper did not pass away until the age of ninety-four, thereby making him both the shortest serving as well as the Prime Minster to have lived the longest life.

Of course, there is a more obvious answer—Campbell is unique in that she was the first, and so far, only female Prime Minister in Canada's history. This fact is highlighted in the rather clumsy title of her memoirs, *Time and Chance: The Political Memoirs of Canada's First Woman Prime Minister.* To the best of my knowledge her memoirs were completed without the aid of a ghostwriter, which suggests that somebody must have been doing their job properly. Still, this is not the answer I had in mind.

Kim Campbell is, to date, the only Prime Minister to have been born in British Columbia—a fact that may soon change.

Though now an established fixture of Southern Ontario, Montblanc was, like myself, born in the sparsely populated Northern Interior of British Columbia, and I suspect that the shared geographical proximity of our birthplaces is part of the reason why he has trusted me to tell the story of his life. Murky idiosyncrasies abound that area and can only be rightly understood by those who have through birth and circumstance unknowingly waded through them. The collegiate hacks and shallow scholars of metropolitan pedigree might study enough to sufficiently mimic the tone and vocabulary, and indeed, they may succeed in accurately describing what the fallen log on the forest floor looks like, but they haven't any idea what kind of creepy crawlies exist underneath that log.

They wouldn't know that it's the type of place where Trooper's seminal 1977 offering, '*We're Here For A Good Time (Not A Long Time)*', could sincerely be somebody's favourite song. The type of place where people did 'favours' for one another with no thought of reciprocation. The type of place where moths were caught and trapped in Tupperware containers to have their wings pulled off and to have boiling water poured on top of them. The type of place where dad's fishing hooks were routinely used to pierce the curious ears of neighbourhood boys in bloody and unsterilized coming-of-age rituals. The type of place where rudderless striplings met in the park after dark to take turns kicking the ribs of the drunk Indians who slept there— whether they wanted to or not. The type of place where touching her would be okay, because enough people were there to witness it and cover for you later. Just do it. Just do it. Just do it. The type of place where the cops knew everyone, and generally allowed folks to settle their own personal matters without their involvement. The type of place where that 'stuttering faggot won't come anywhere near her ever again.' The type of place where self-imposed penance wasn't valued as social currency. The type of place where a four-story leap from the tallest building in town should be avoided, as it wouldn't necessarily be enough to finish the job.

Though Montblanc's youth differed from my own in many ways, we've both been baptized by the frigid waters of the Fraser and we've both been partially formed by the chemical compounds it carries. As such, I have an inherent insight into his mind that few else will have. I can only believe that this is why

I'm here. Anyone with a rudimentary understanding of language and structure can slap together a man's biography. But who else can empathize with the facts on a phenomenological level and present them as such, save for those who never had to learn them in the first place?

Monty warns me against dwelling too long on his childhood in B.C. or over-romanticizing his appreciation for the province. He thinks that might isolate readers from the rest of the country. 'Pander to populous places' he says. Always demonstrating foresight, always thinking ahead. Still, while he's now some 3500 kilometers away from that place and has been for quite some time, I do occasionally sense in him a wistful nostalgia. I would say it's nostalgia for simpler days, but that's too easy and not entirely accurate. Though I've only known him a short while Montblanc has yet to strike me as a man burdened with any serious regrets. So why then does this notoriously stoic and driven champion of enterprise sporadically emit a faint scent of remorse?

That is something that I just don't know, though I do have one idea:

There are some truly terrible sins that occur in rural British Columbia after dark, but none are more frightening than those that occur during broad daylight in the offices and boardrooms of the cities.

# POLLARDING

IF ALL YOU knew about Maxime Montblanc was based on what you've read in this book, you might justifiably be wondering how a man of his eccentricity and mercuriality has attained and maintained the positions that he has. Suffice it to say that the man I see behind closed doors and under the artificial lighting of private hours is not the same man that so effortlessly commands the boardrooms of public perception. Out there in the real world M is a true master of his crafts. I wager he's tried making love while listening to *The Blue Danube*. But this is not what the public thinks about when they gaze upon the weathered Adonis with his fancy words and soothing voice and perfect delivery.

Monsieur Montblanc's public speeches have been criticized as needlessly verbose and prior to meeting him I assumed this was a deliberate rhetorical act. The thing is, he is in fact *less* elegant when he speaks to the public. While my purple words are the result of deliberately inflated overcompensation, his are entirely genuine. Still, when you speak with him he brings the entirety of his focus and empathy. I suspect this has partially contributed to his political and financial success. He has a way of ensuring that he is the most important person in any given room while still being able to process and carefully respond to every word spoken to him.

Monty made his millions and won his seat and built the empire of his name almost entirely on his supernatural awareness. I know the federal election is still some time away, but the pundits and bloggers are already predicting his victory. This wasn't a lifelong dream of his. He wasn't a starry-eyed child who wanted to grow up to become the Prime Minister. This is an opportunity he noticed well into his adult life and is now planning to act on. An exclamation point at the end of his life's résumé.

You can tell a lot about a person by how they respond to people who are better than they are. Some people get defensive or antagonistic or jealous, some become sycophantic or overtly deferential just to remain in the orbit of their superiors, some try to learn as much as they can and analyze the template of success before them. By any standard societal definition, Montblanc is better than most people. I myself am not a man of substantial ambition. I never intended to be a leader of any kind. I thought my life would be a resounding success if I could see my hobby of writing through to any tangible recognition or financial gain. M, the better man, has provided this opportunity. And how am I to respond? Take for instance our conversation at breakfast this morning. He tells me:

"I've read *Resorting Conviction*. You're an excellent writer."

I thank him, but I don't have time to internalize the compliment before he continues.

"But you are a terrible businessman. I know what the Premier paid you to write that for him, but have you any idea how much *he* made from it? Without my protection you would be devoured."

And my baron is at once all things of beauty and sin in this life. He is the boatman at world's end ferrying the chosen few across the moribund morass. With the monosyllabic first words spoken by primitive man came the first lies, the first acts of knavery and manipulation given form. And thus was his shovel given a handle and his momentum propelled forward. He tickles the *Turkish March* without missing a note. I drink his coffee and I think it's the best I've ever had, as if he grew and processed the beans himself with the same care and proficiency he displays in all his endeavors. It gives me the energy I need to translate his deeds into words so that other might share in venerating the man we were all meant to be. He is a master of his crafts people.

At one point in his life he liked them young. She was eighteen at a time he was nearly twice that. He told me the that the last time he remembered feeling jealousy was when she confessed that she was also seeing someone who just happened to be one year older than he was. That was nearly twenty years ago. Are we really to believe that he hasn't felt the tap of jealousy on his shoulder once since then? Oh, but the men worth reading about are not the men who routinely do believable things now, are they? No, I don't believe that either, but that's what I'll need to convince myself of if I want to do this properly. It's method acting. I must look upon his as the work of God and mine as the scribe who is to finish curating the Bible before binding it with blood and skin.

It's just that sometimes I feel so very low in myself. Surely so must he?

## II

# Plaudits

"An unexpectedly raw account from a notoriously divisive public figure . . . *Restoring Conviction* portrays the former Premier not sympathetically or critically, but in a simple and refreshingly honest way."
— Jeff Malay, *Toronto Citizen*

"Eloquently written, the memoirs of Canada's most controversial Premier may not do much to redeem him, but that doesn't mean they aren't an absolute pleasure to read."
— J. J. Ricard, *Montreal Sun*

"A must-read, not just for those interested in the occasionally esoteric world of Canadian politics, but for anyone interested in a genuine, occasionally heartbreaking, and above all, a thoroughly human story."
— Lisa Tennant, *Vancouver Herald*

"No stranger to controversy or criticism, the oft-discussed actions and decisions of the former Premier are laid bare here . . . *Restoring Conviction* presents the fascinating story straight from the source with no punches pulled."
— R. Michel, *Gazette de Quebec*

"Stunning an engrossing . . . *Restoring Conviction* may have just single-handedly breathed life into the dying genre of Canadian political memoirs."

— Jon Shermann, *The National Mail*

# Pabulum

So this is it for me then? Confined to write the biographies of greater men for the rest of my pitiful little life? Am I the true twenty-first century cuckold, left to burn incense in sin while insincere seers sense inside the silent searing of my pride? Telling the stories of others while telling none of my own? My life's work fluttering on and invisibly infecting the legacy of people whose names are worth remembering while I float unnoticeably down the Columbia toward the safe obscurity of the Pacific? I have stories too.

I've long been a lover of bread and could happily eat it unaccompanied and isolated. Most of my life I've never had the kind of money to eat at the types of restaurants that offer free bread. Once (the summer of 2013 for the future historians who would waste *their* lives documenting my own), while ceremoniously indulging with my unintended like the responsible consumers she wanted us to be, we were presented with the pre-meal bread, warm from the oven and nestled meticulously in an adorable woven basket. Four beautiful pieces for the two of us, the mathematics wonderfully parallel though compromised when I managed to finish three pieces before she her first. 'Don't rip it, use the knife.' Her words heard but not processed as I chewed faster than I could swallow. Oh, sweet divinity, embrace me with your doughy arms and lift me from the ticking perils of consciousness. Cindy, yes, that was our server's name. 'Would you two care for some more bread?' Why, yes, we would Cindy! And certainly some more after that! I see the tendrils of embarrassment starting to tickle the neck of my dinner companion. She didn't want this. She wanted to wear her best dress. She wanted me to sit up straight and make gentle conversation about the wine, and how it was good, but not quite as good as the stuff we had at the vineyard in the Okanagan that one time. She wanted to play grown-up. I hadn't yet reached the point where I felt like telling her that all wine tasted like shit to me, but as I recall that conversation was not too far off. Deep within me, buried under the black troches of contempt I had been routinely swallowing, there resided a genuine will to follow script and maintain the soft smile I knew would come upon her predictable face, but not tonight. Not with bread this remarkable and an appetite as unrewarded as mine. Cindy, I just can't seem to get enough of this tremendous bread. Do us a favour and bring out another basket if you don't mind. Oh, and my regards to the chef. The chef doesn't make the bread you say? Well belay that order then. Thank you, Cindy, you're doing a bang-up job. I'm eating louder and more furiously with each piece I conquer. I've hit the double digits. If I wasn't on a date I think I could have broken the world record because *fuck me* this bread is good. Don't you think so, babe? She's checking her phone now. Trying not to pay me much attention, but that's okay, everyone else in the restaurant has her covered. Eventually the main course came. I don't think I finished it. It was pretty good but probably not worth the meal's $120 price tag. Not to mention the other non-monetary costs that were incurred.

Maybe my life isn't worth knowing. Maybe they don't need to put out a casting call for someone to play me in the movie version. Maybe I'm better off accepting my earthly duty of presenting the stories of others for pennies and not for praise.

Though I do occasionally lie awake wondering what Cindy ever made of her life.

## 13

## PSELLISM

I'M FINDING IT hard to write about Big White at the moment. He left the basement office about twenty minutes ago but I've since failed to climb back on board the old train car of progress. Today's visit was brief, though with lasting implications that I did not intend to be still wrestling with. See, I don't particularly like to be mired in my own thoughts. I'm a fall-asleep-with-the-TV-on kind of guy. I can do without the moments of existential panic that accompany dark and quiet rooms. No sir, I wouldn't last five minutes under the Bodhi Tree. But that can't be my fault. Surely I'm a victim of generational circumstance? Goal-oriented. Maybe that's a better way of looking at it. I don't mind climbing mountains so long as I never make it to the top. Yes, I truly am the champion of modern millennials everywhere, my finger placed firmly on the pulse of my successor milieu and the millions of voices that comprise it. So many voices, so many words, so many stories and experiences to draw from.

So why couldn't I honestly answer a simple question?

Living within M's gravitational pull has been quite the adjustment thus far. One of the many oddities that I've now come to expect are the string of unusual questions that he insists on asking me. They come unannounced and are difficult to predict, though I don't necessarily mind answering them honestly, even when they are of a deeply personal nature and even when it doesn't seem like he wants me to answer them in the first place. Back in the real world the level of privacy that I normally maintain would be the stuff of legends—if it weren't for the level of privacy that I normally maintain—but with M, there exists a precocious openness that allows me to provide unmasked responses to questions I would typically dread. I'm not sure what to attribute this to. Maybe it's because I know this is only a temporary arrangement with an eventual end point. Maybe it's because I'm unwittingly imitating the openness that he himself displays. Maybe it's because there's a pay-day on the horizon that I'm willing to jump through all sorts of hoops to ensure. Regardless, I haven't lost any sleep over his questions. Quite the opposite, I've found engaging in strange acts of unencumbered honesty to be quite liberating. I haven't yet felt the compulsion or need to lie to Montblanc like I so often do with others.

Until about twenty minutes ago.

Our meeting today was brief and strictly about the book, but as he stood up to leave the room he paused a moment before asking his entirely unrelated question:

"How do you envision yourself in a happy future?"

And what did I tell him? After taking some time to contemplate his words I eventually told him that in my happy future I see myself dancing with a woman. I told him that this was a daydream I often had, something I would think about before falling asleep at night. I told him that in these visions I was dressed in well-fitted black and white dancewear, and my partner in a grey gown. I told him that when we danced, everyone else was entranced by our faultless movements. In grace and sameness we moved our forms noiselessly across the floor. I told him that I can't see her face, but I know that she is happy. And so am I. So happy that my body has transcended the incoordination and shyness that once kept it imprisoned, so happy that for once I didn't mind having all of the eyes in the room on me. I told him that in my visions the dance never ended. I never let it. I didn't want to know what happened after that because there's no way it could have been as perfect as that moment was. I told him that this is my vision of future happiness, one where I have learned to be loved, one where I have learned to step out of my own limitations.

But none of this was true. This answer that I had provided was entirely fabricated and was delivered with just enough authenticity to sufficiently please M and end the conversation.

And so, I've been sitting her for the last twenty minutes thinking on his question and wondering why I felt the need to lie about my answer. But here I am, ready to submit to you now in a selfish attempt to placate the echoing caws of guilt, the truth, as I understand it.

***

Before walking onto the makeshift stage and taking my podium, I sneak a quick glance toward the eager crowd. There's a turnout that the owners and organizers are very excited about. 'Substantial' they call it. A lot of work has been done to organize this event. All of it for me. They even used the colour scheme I requested. I'm comfortable and relaxed when I am finally introduced to smiles and applause. Stepping behind the podium, I see my fans enthusiastically clapping with a copy of my new book nestled safely under their armpits as I open my own copy to Chapter Thirteen and begin reading the carefully arranged words contained within. And oh, how I read! I read fluid and flawless with furious and fortuitous fortitude. I don't need to change a single word. I don't need to be obsessively aware of the hard consonants or alliterations creeping up the page. I read elegantly and with a confident and attractive tonality. My words, unerringly transcribed from print to speech, resound with the captivated crowd. I finish the chapter to the sounds of admiration and acceptance. I don't need to apologize for time wasted. I don't need to politely nod to the disingenuous and once-expected chorus of, 'you did so well', 'it was barely noticeable', 'you're so brave.'

And now a line forms as I take my seat at the table that has been set up meticulously and lovingly for me. I converse with my fans and answer questions as I take my time elaborately signing their books. My book. 'Who should I make this out to?' 'I'm glad you picked up on that'. 'No, that character wasn't based on a real person'. 'You want to do what with me? That's very flattering miss, but this is an all-ages event.' Well I guess my time is up. Thank you all so much.

Thank you all so much, but my time is up.

My time is up.

And now I'm back in my ninth grade English class, pouring my entire being over the latest assignment. 'Prepare and deliver a five-minute speech on a topic of your choice.' A visceral dread envelops me as Mr. Smith eventually calls my name. When I take this podium I am neither relaxed nor comfortable. My hands shake uncontrollably as I place my well-prepared and routinely rehearsed notes in front of me. What follows is what I assume to be the longest and most difficult five minutes that my classmates have ever experienced. In the few brief instances when I'm able to tear my sheepish eyes away from my notes and toward the jury, I see Mr. Smith using his own to tacitly encourage me. Eventually I stumble over the finish line and everyone claps. Everyone fucking claps as if by some miracle of God I was able to finish. Except I didn't finish at all. I had to skip about half of my speech just to fit the time. And I tried. I really tried. I researched, I revised, I endeavored to write an amazing speech and I practiced it again and again, just to be introduced to the refrains I would soon come to know by heart, 'you did so well', 'it was barely noticeable', 'you're so brave.'

***

And now I'm back to where I am, with all that I want to be still far away from me. Caught betwixt a daydream fantasy and a repressed memory, when I should be free of both, toiling away and searching for the words to fill a book that isn't my own. Searching for the words that have always transitioned so easily from thought to pen, though never again to be spoken from behind any of the perilous podiums I've known.

## 14

## Pantheon

Sometimes when M reveals to me his frustrations with the demagoguery he is often expected to engage in, I start seeing him less like a man and more like a God. Or maybe it was the other way around. He recently told me that he thought his devoutly Catholic parents were merely faking their piety as means of further distinguishing themselves from the English Protestant majority that they were surrounded by when they relocated to British Columbia just prior to his birth. He believed it was a sort of identity claim. As I understand it, despite being raised in a strictly French Catholic household Maxime himself did not develop any significant lasting religious convictions—unless he was in public. Though far less outwardly vocal about his faith than many of his political peers, there were nevertheless times when he was encouraged to strike those hymnal chords.

I myself do not adhere to any modern form of spiritual practice or belief, though sometimes at the very late hours, when my mind can afford to wander, I can't help but dwell on the possibility that my soul is somehow tied to the will and divine mission of the fertility deities of old . . .

*Ishtar*

Here, the First Mother and giver of Life. I submit myself wholly. I will drink your bath water and ruminate for a separate lifetime on each of your individual vertebra. Allow me to lick clean the impious dirt clinging to your explicit form. Small women surround you in wordless reverence, stick-like figures applying oils concocted from the sacrificial tears and semen of your devout congregation. Each of your legs wider than my frame, seventeen sins apart, and I remain head-bowed and humbled at your feet, still stained from the vermilion tincture of those who fell from between your legs too soon and too eager in their purpose. The armies of the East, rumbling in the distance, will be stayed by these hands—else granted be my death. No, Ishtar, so long as I breathe, never shall they enjoy the gift of your proximity. My eyes are open and my strength well-endowed enough that I might tear them away from your figure and toward the dangers that conspire to take you from us.

### Aphrodite

The ruinous future will not evade us. We met in jest, and so forever it would remain, if only it were in my power to dictate. Pray laughter may again return to the faithful. Hold still while your flesh be pierced, we must make the markings now. In the contemptuous year that will be 2014, they will serve as your only reliable means of identification. I will meet you then and you will draw from me a force shot so high that even Uranus must take notice. Until then I remain the vigil keeper of your dormant state, our secret of lust and redness cordially kept.

But under what name and guise?

No, for they are coming.

### Qetesh

Born of incestuous union under scattered stars and summer sky, my Lordess waits patiently for me to mutter my binding oath. Thousands of slaves assembled to witness the flowing crimson let free from my borrowed veins and collected in the ceremonial chalice. Too many eyes make for unsteady nerves. No direction to run. I taste the indecency in the air as she beckons me toward her chambers. Four men stand at the door, another two by her bed, though not a single one of them blocks my path. Reparations for my sins is it? Memories of these transgressions to travel 3200 years and inhabit this body? To write this book? With no female characters named? Think of the critics. Think of yourself more importantly. Can such a fate be avoided by lying with the exposed deity before me? By letting free my member and savagery with no thoughts of shame or remorse? Witness now the symmetry of her lips and the evenness of her eyes, a surprise given the disgusting nature of her genealogy. I hold my breath as I enter her, my final sin.

### Xochiquetzal

She stands in a field of lavender. There is no consensus in the academic world regarding when lavender was first introduced into the New World, or if in fact it was ever introduced at all. I myself thought this sight to be a touch anachronistic, but what good are superficial ponderings in the company of such a combination of beauty? Never mind the usurpation of the hitherto monochromatic palette in place, let this purple presence root deep in my cerebrum and make an automaton out of me. She pulls a piece from the ground and places the root between her lips. I have, in this exact moment, become her messiah and my volition in my mission is now crystalline. Through her gates I will walk, one head held high and the other chaffed and bruised. I am not yet emptied my love. Let us paint these purple fields with our juices. Red and white and now a softer shade of purple.

### Leonard Cohen

Teach me to speak.
Teach me to feel.
Teach me to fuck.
Teach me to kneel.

## 15

## PERNOCTATION

I'VE SPENT ENOUGH nights in Montblanc's guest bedroom that it is now beginning to feel more like my own. From when I lie down to when I fall asleep there's a noiseless and unpaved backroad of time where I am free to piece together flashes of M's life in some kind of workable way. With every logistical concern that is pruned more inconsequential roots break through the ground and struggle to catch some light. Does Max sing with fervor the words of *O Canada* or does he simply mouth them? I'm a terrible judge of character but I do read a lot.

Still, there are no words in the lexicon that seem readily obvious when attempting to truthfully define Maxime Montblanc. He intimidates me while at the same time putting me at ease. He insults me while he lavishes me with praise. He changes roles seamlessly from mentor to villain, from an object of contempt to one of pity. He fluctuates between profound insights and arbitrary vulgarities. He never uses curse words. He's a poet and he's a preacher but when he speaks I don't know whether to scribe his every word for fear that they may be lost or to burst out laughing at the utter ridiculousness of his overreliance on archaic and grandiose language. His eyes project an unwavering confidence while alluding to some sadness whitewashed and eroded to a lingering essence. The story I've been paid to convey is the insipid journey of a self-made man who came from nothing and rose to a position of political prominence and leadership. If told with conventional language, strategic focus, and occasional embellishment, I suspect that its shallow feelgoodery will have the result and impact Maxime intends. But that's hardly the entire story. My position affords me peeks into his life and with every—hold on.

There's someone in the backyard. It's a clouded and lightless night, but through the window above the bed I can see a faint silhouetted figure standing amid the darkness. My chest runs tight and hot as the cogs of some rusted fight-or-flight mechanism begin turning inside me. I strain my eyes at the human-shaped mass and it stands there motionless, but it stands there all the same. I avoid making any movements in the hope that I may remain unseen. I can't be certain for how long it really was but after forming and swallowing a lump in my throat another figure enters stage left. This large body I recognize immediately as Montblanc's. As my eyes slowly adjust to the dark I see the two men shake hands. If they are speaking they are doing so too softly for me to hear. Less than a minute passes before I see Montblanc place his hand kindly on the stranger's shoulder and pat it three times before turning around to leave. The stranger exits in the opposite direction and disappears into the trees. I listen intently but I never hear Montblanc come back inside the house. I lie awake for some time with a dormant and inaudacious mind before sleep arrives.

★★★

I dream of a horse that has been placed under my care. The horse is lame, and he slams his body against brick walls and he collapses in exhaustion after being ridden for only a short distance. His heart beat is pronounced and audible. I sense the horse is famished and I lead him into a field of tall grass but he refuses to eat, instead he falls onto his side. I look around the dying field for a moment before I lie down beside him, my head resting inches away from the violent pounding of his chest.

★★★

In the morning I have breakfast with M and I think long on whether I should bring up what I saw the previous night. There's a guilt of potentially knowing something that I was not meant to know and revealing my hand might be the only means of alleviating it.

"Duh-duh-duh diiiid I suh-suh-see you in the back yuh-yuh-yard last nnnnight?"

His expression changes, though I don't possess the skill to articulate how.

"I don't know, Lawrence. Did you see me in the backyard last night?"

"I think sssso. There was suh-suh-sommme-someone else too."

"And so it would appear then as if you had the answer to your question well before you decided to ask it. Surely I haven't enlisted you under my employ to waste words so? You were meant to do the exact opposite as I recall."

"I was just wuh-wuh-wuh-wondering about—"

"You were just wondering about things that are beyond your required understanding. I'll not claim you a liar or attempt to discount what you may have seen but nor will I offer any explanation beyond those that you might of your own volition fathom. And now if you will excuse me, the day beckons. I expect you will be wanting to start work as well."

As Montblanc gets up from the table and carries his empty plate to the kitchen his arms begin to shake and I hear his fork clattering against the porcelain as he leaves the room. A few scattered possibilities burn through. Maybe it was some sort of drug deal? No, that's small-time thinking. To the best of my knowledge Max isn't a user, and even if he was, he's a powerful man with access to any vice he desires; he wouldn't need to subject himself to shady midnight dealings. Maybe he was soliciting the assassination of a rival? No, that's thinking a little too freely. Of course he has enemies but that's not how problems are handled in the real world. Unless that's what they want me to think? Before I can explore any more asinine scenarios I see M opening the front door to leave. Before he walks out he stops in the doorframe and without turning around to face me he offers a parting gift of sorts.

"There are mysteries in this life that are indeed worth exploring. And explore them I might if aught it were in my capacities to do. Strychnine is bitter to be sure, but inelegant and ultimately outclassed by the weight of your words. Cherish them thusly."

## 16

# PENUMBRA

FOGGY BACKSEATS AND a concealed waxing crescent. Please, she's overdone it this time. Others too. Like the same disc we've been listening to now only one track shy of starting its fourth go-round. Never seen these hours this way before. Never known better. Sneaking my head closer to hers, every motion a victory. Please, she's overdone it this time. Neighbourhood streets to nowhere, specked with concrete abutments, the immovable, walk-over-able markers of progress. Not sure under this light. This was when one spoke only in absolutes. The sky was never falling in, despite the eyewitness testimony to the contrary. Fixed from the start. Please, she's overdone it. Intimately familiar with the underused ashtray, anachronistic signifiers. Acceptance now—you won't be getting out of bed until early afternoon at best. Small agreements, justifications, the maiden voyage of the 'special night' clause. Written in hope, written with the expectation of a gambler. I'll be there. Maybe not now, but I've handed my shiny marble to Mr. Rube Goldberg and now I can wait. Sitting on my hands. Arm falling asleep. Best not to move. Best not to disturb the sanctity of the arrangement. Stay still like a picture. Keep this pose forever. This was when one spoke only in absolutes.

I confess to nothing because I'm innocent.

Hmm, not quite.

I *choose* to confess to nothing because I'm innocent.

No, try this one:

I am confessing to nothing *because* I am innocent.

Okay, but what about this?

I'm innocent, and as such, I have nothing to confess.

Wrap it up already.

I have nothing to confess, though my innocence is open to interpretation.

Yeah, that's the one.

## 17

# POLTROON

REFLECTING ON FAILURES today, and why not? When there's so much to be happy about the temptation to ask my friends Regret and Shame to double-up on the other side of the seesaw becomes too strong. I, in my infinite wisdom and generosity, only wish to share my profundity with those closest to me. Tips on becoming a productive member of society: 1) avoid clocks with audible ticks, 2) wear shoes that match the occasion, 3) periodically dwell on past failures, embarrassments, and unfulfilled aspirations. The finale of this triad now beyond appeased on this late and languid morn. In the tenth grade Michaela Flores paid me twenty bucks to write her a short story for her English class. Alas, Michaela, notoriously amoral and destined to perpetually graze the fetid fields of unremarkability. With eyes affixed to the floor I accepted her proposition. The story was well-received and Michaela earned an A. Cut to fifteen years later and count the circumstantial similarities. Devourer of life, do not go hungry on my blank *curriculum vitae,* let me offer to you a nourishing alternative worthy of consumption. The parsing and cataloguing of Mister Maxime Magnificent. All the angel's blessings on the ground he walks. At fifteen M would partially spend his summers with his parents, largely unsupervised, at their rented cabin on Tisdall Lake. A majestic memory meriting mention in Montblanc's marvelous memoirs. What gets left out is the fact that he used to sneak out at night to fuck the daughter of the guy who ran the campsite down the way. At fifteen I was writing a short story for Michaela Flores in the hope that she might let me touch her. No grace allowed through my windpipe, so no invitation for her to touch my 'puh-puh-puh-puh-puh-puh-puh-puh', forcing me to rely instead on my precocious affinity toward arranging and aligning the proper phrases on paper, translated from carnal thought to pen. Don't scoff. I wasn't the only one. If it redeems me I'll happily mention that my libido, much like the list of my professional accomplishments, is as dry as flaky apple pie. Continuing the tradition of doing things wrong, folded and inconspicuously slipped, promptly ignored, and I sleep only after blaming the fashions of the time and choking the piece Father Munroe said I oughtn't to. In the rare instances when Regret and Shame had conflicting schedules, I continued to write short stories. Not for the promises of meager sums of money or requited lust, but out of genuine enthusiasm. At age twenty-two I submitted for publication a collection of these stories. Roundly rejected. I'm allergic to structure and plot, they say. Stories need arcs and characters need growth and I don't know anything about that. At age twenty-two Montblanc was a few months away from becoming a self-made millionaire. That's because he is a natural winner. Not like us. Keen historians like myself may pinpoint his first steps on the path to victory, and indeed I have. In third grade (making him around eight years old), Montblanc won the position of class mayor in an exercise designed to teach young minds the merits and mechanics of democracy. An excellent anecdote for the book that will emphasize his natural ability to lead. What will be left out is the fact that Montblanc's primary 'competition', a gangly kid named Tony, was something of a dud. Lacking the charisma and social gifts of Montblanc, Tony was destined to lose from the start. In secret, the two of them made a deal. 'If you vote for me, I'll vote for you.' They both made this promise yet when the votes were counted Tony received not a single one. Some of us are just natural winners. As for the rest of you, I cordially invite you to join Tony and I at the loser's table. Regret and Shame will be arriving shortly. Remember to bring appropriate footwear. At age twenty-seven I was spending my nights on a mattress in the corner of my room when I was offered the opportunity of a lifetime by the former Premier—ghostwrite his memoirs. My name was recommended for the job by a former professor who praised my attention to detail and my 'natural

sounding literary voice.' They were released to near-unanimous
critical praise, and more importantly, they were read by many
people. Still, my name was nowhere near them. At age twenty-
seven, and about thirteen years away from becoming an MP,
Montblanc was the CEO of a company responsible for about 400
jobs. By this time he had permanently relocated to Southern
Ontario to be closer to Canada's business and political epicenter.
That's the decision of an undeniable winner. Shadows can't
move in the dark. They too are bound by the rules of the natural
world. I can count on one reddened hand the number of women
who have let me inside them. Is M at all concerned that the
daughter of the guy who ran the campsite down the way might
speak to the press about their summer night trysts on the shores
of Tisdall Lake? Or any of the others for that matter, numbering
in the triple digits as I understand it? He recognizes no problems
born from these unions. 'If anything, that would only serve to
bring me more votes.' Oh, Great White Mountain! How attuned
to the heartbeat of humanity you are! The natural shepherd of the
confused flock. Bombastic bravado and braggadocio seeping
through your perfect pores. Today, at age thirty, I've a collection
of poems and short stories unpublished and unread. On a scale of
remedial to Leonard Cohen, the average of them falls within the
'faded denim' range.

I don't dare to describe or distinguish my discarded discord
or discolouration—deep down, drawing distinct and disguised
drafts of delectable decoctions and counting my options, I see the
faintest hint of light. The shadows begin moving again. Who—
heaven save me—who owns the hands reaching from above to
pull me to safety? They look friendly and familiar to these
strained and glassy eyes of mine. Oh, my dearest friends! I knew
you wouldn't abandon me to these closing caverns!

And as the cracked hand of Regret and the supple hand of
Shame pull me to safety, I knew in that brilliant moment that I
would never be alone.

# PRORATION

M. M. M. HAD RECENTLY adopted the habit of skipping all attempts at introductory formality when making his semi-regular appearances in my office. My office? I've never had an office in my life. It's his house, it's his office. Maybe I'm getting a little too comfortable here. The onset of Stockholm syndrome perhaps? Don't think too hard about that. Don't think too hard about anything beyond the immediate. 'One day at a time' as the newly free apparently say. Anyway, he arrived fully suited and seemingly ready to make the public appearance he was undoubtedly dressed for, save for the newspaper he carried in his left hand, folded in half and opened to a specific story. There was something endearing about the fact that Monty still read the newspaper in the morning. I couldn't quite place it, but I took a small comfort in knowing that the unshakeable mountain of a man may be, by just a hair, a touch out of sync with this brave modern world of ours. And I would always have that on him. Without any attempt at verbal foreplay he begins reading.

"A community firestorm erupted after a fifteen-year-old girl was filmed engaging in sexual acts with as many as two dozen boys in a bathroom at Oshawa's Elm Bay High School. The girl allegedly invited one boy into the bathroom to have intercourse, and soon after several other boys entered the bathroom to watch and to engage in sexual activities with the girl. Several of the observers took pictures and videos of the events, many of which would later circulate on the Internet and social media. No legal or disciplinary actions have been taken as of yet, though the school's principal has said that she is working with witnesses and law enforcement officials to 'get the facts straight' before making any decisions regarding punishment."

Montblanc tosses the paper onto the empty seat in front of the desk and directs his attention to me for the first time since entering the room. Without waiting for my response, he begins his performance.

"Shame her. Shame her until she doesn't want to live anymore. Shame her so that she, and any others who would emulate her reprehensible behaviour, know full well that we, as a civilized and decent society, will not tolerate such vulgarity. Most of those boys were on the hockey team. They were good kids who got carried away in the moment. But this girl needs to be made an example of. Let us all shame her in unison for corrupting the moral fibre of our great city!"

My head tilts to the side and the ever-perceptive politician picks up on my expression of bewilderment.

"Perhaps a shade too zealous? Indeed, it is hard to justify the call for a witch hunt these days. Trying times aren't they? I'll likely not be asked to comment on this story, though seeing as how it did occur within my district it is always important to have a piece prepared just in case. Still, I seem to be having more trouble than usual in formulating the correct response. Blaming the girl is sure to backfire, though defending her may indicate a lapse in moral order. A finicky one this. What say you, Lawrence?"

"Is, is, is she okay?"

"Come again?"

"The g-guh-guh-girl, is she, is she, is she okay?"

"Oh sweet friend, how unparalleled our priorities."

## 19

## Panglossianism

THIS MIGHT BE the nicest day I've ever seen, and by gum, I've seen a few. These clear Oshawa summer skies make a guy's head spin with fancy ideas that might seem scary had they not been baking all day. Maybe it does get better than this, but I'll leave those questions to greedy gazers with more sophisticated vocabularies. Who can sit inside and write on a day like this? I have a daily word quota I need to hit but wouldn't you know it, it's just not coming. Maybe I can blitz through the rest of this chapter and get to seizing what's left of this day. All work and no play, right?

*'And so it was that Maxime Magnificent Montblanc bought, bullied, and bonked his way to the top of the political food chain—and all was well in his glorious kingdom of Canada.'*

Wonderful penmanship, old chap! No, wrong word. Penmanship refers to the aesthetic quality of the physical writing itself, and remember, your physical writing looks worse than you sound when you try to say that Peter Piper thing. Zing! But please stop making fun of yourself, it's not fair, you know all of your weaknesses. Regardless, the penmanship is irrelevant because it's not there. People type on computers these days.

Come to think of it, that reminds me of something. This is somewhat tangential and only relevant to purists who insist on reading every word on each page in sequential order, so skip this paragraph if you need to be somewhere soon. Still here? Okay, so toward the end of his life, Nietzsche's eyesight was beginning to fail and he found it difficult to focus on writing the old-fashioned way—that's pen-to-paper for any precocious youngsters who happen to be reading this. As a refresher,

Nietzsche was that old German philosopher that people new to philosophy often think is the greatest philosopher to ever philosophize. The truth? He was okay. Anyway, to compensate for these difficulties Nietzsche acquired for himself a typewriter and starting doing his writing on that. The typewriter allowed him to continue working, but it has been suggested that when he started using the machine, the style of his writing shifted noticeably. It became tighter and more surgical. More mechanical. Something to think about, people.

As for my writing, well, it's shit. Maybe I need a new typewriter. But who cares? There's more important things in life. That sun out there is smiling directly at me, practically begging me to enjoy its company. How do you turn that down? Are there any beaches in this shit town? Shit, I shouldn't have said that. This is a great town. Seriously. No disrespect intended. So, to the nearby beach of Lake Ontario then? I mean, that's fine . . . It is the smallest of the Great Lakes, but whatever. Still bigger than most lakes, I guess. Do I have a bathing suit here? More importantly, is my body bathing suit ready? The sands of Lake Ontario are as good a place as any to meet the one.

Yeah, I can see it now. She's sunbathing on a floral towel and she's wearing one of those floppy sun hats. She's wearing sunglasses that obscure most of her face, but I can still tell that underneath she's a special kind of pretty. She's wearing a black two-piece bathing suit and you can tell that she doesn't regularly skip leg day at the gym. Okay, no. You just ruined it, that's disgusting. You could have just said 'she's attractive' and left it at that. Don't focus on her appearance, if she really is the one she probably has more going on than just her looks. Oh, what's this? She's brought a book with her. Who is she reading? McCarthy? That's sexy but not realistic. No one in history has ever brought McCarthy to the beach. It doesn't matter. She sees me emerge from the water and she calls to me. She says:

'Hey cowboy, a little help?'

And then she throws me a bottle of sunscreen and uses her thumb to point to her back.

No, cut! Have you ever listened to people talk before? Nobody would ever say that. Let's just skip ahead to the part where we're making sandcastles on the beach. No, that's not a euphemism, we're actually making sandcastles and I'm even resisting the temptation to tell her that she's doing it wrong and the structural integrity of her castle's walls are compromised because of it. Because in this fantasy I'm only a shitty person on the inside. After sandcastles, we go to the quaint little ice cream parlour nearby that for decades has been the go-to first date location for uncreative people. I get myself a single scoop of vanilla and she—no, stop right there. You don't order vanilla. You're not eighty. Order something that has a bit of character. Okay fine, I get myself a single scoop of, I don't know, rum raisin? Oh, sweet lord I'm pathetic. Whatever, the flavour doesn't matter. She eats hers from a colourful paper bowl because she doesn't like cones. Wait, what kind of person doesn't like cones? Are we sure she's the one? She uses a little plastic spoon that would make anyone holding it look adorable. When she's finished eating I take the spoon home to keep as a memento of our time together. No, you're ruining it again. That's just weird. Skip to the end already.

We've been married forty years. She brought home rum raisin ice cream even though I *very specifically* asked for vanilla. She 'forgot' to get cones too. The only thing keeping me going now is the hope that she might die before me so I can at least have a few days without her.

Yup, she's the one all right.

Well that was fun if only a bit farfetched. A more accurate depiction of my potential day at the beach would involve me gauchely sitting in the dirt by myself as people younger and more attractive than me throw a Frisbee to each other while using words that I don't know the meaning to. 'Mommy, what's that guy doing here by himself?' Yes, mommy, what can you tell us about that guy? And all this would last for about thirty minutes before I convince myself that I've had enough sun for the day and slink myself back to the safety net that is M's house.

At this point I need to ask if it's normal for daydream fantasies to end as starkly as mine often seem to. I suppose it saves me the trouble of having to go out and live it for myself. I mean, it is a nice day and all but is it *that* nice that I need to skip out on writing to go try my luck at some beach that I'm not familiar with? From a purely statistical perspective the chances that I'll meet the one there are negligible. Still, it might be nice to just turn off the old thinker and soak up some sun for a change. It might even be fun. Hell, maybe I'll get some ice cream too. A *double* scoop. Of something crazy. Something like . . . I don't know, tiger? That's a thing, right? Yeah, to hell with it! You should take chances once in a while. Sometimes you have to give in to spontaneity to really feel alive. Wayne Gretzky said that you miss one hundred percent of the shots that you don't take and, dammit, I'm going to take this shot! I'm going to get out there and enjoy this gorgeous day that's been gifted to me from on high! I'm going to—

And it was right at that moment that Montblanc entered the room.

## 20

# PARASITIZATION

CURIOUSLY CURT, MONTBLANC greets me with a surgically focused inquiry purposefully impervious to misinterpretation.

"How much of my book have you written today?"

I feel a chain drag across my chest as I come to the quick realization that the answer to that question is not the correct one.

"Hi Muh–Muh–Mmmmax, I, I was actually just about t-t-to, to, to start, I just needed t—"

"Do you know what your problem is, Larry Mann?"

A hesitation on my part. Though I am fine-tuned to the frequency of my problems to the point of disassociation, I don't answer, knowing full well that the mountainous mammoth of a man is about to play my part for me.

"You are a parasite. You are a broken and incomplete organism listlessly floating through your existence until you stumble upon the lifeblood of an unsuspecting host, an oasis of soon evaporated opportunity where you may continue your insipid journey into meaninglessness. You are a paltry creature, sucking the vitality out of higher-functioning forms until there is nothing left. What type of existence is this?"

Harsh, but he's not wrong. I'm surprised at my ability to maintain eye contact as he continues.

"I'm no longer fond of parasites. There are too many of them and their welcome has been roundly overstayed. I feel them in my hair, tearing it out strand by strand with invisible force. I feel them in my eyes, usurping the vision that I once had for this country. I feel them in my lungs, stealing my oxygen, leaving only just enough to keep me sustained. I feel them in my testicles, picking off my sperm one by one and replacing them with doppelgangers. And why haven't you written anything today? Do you intend to fight with the others over the prime real estate of my body? I ask again, what type of existence is this?"

His body and tone soften slightly as he shifts into a story.

"I had an employee once, a manager type. A weak man. A parasite. The time had long since come for him to go, but understand, I was a blinder person then. A more forgiving person. His pitiful cries and assurances pierced me. 'Mr. Montblanc, please give me another chance, I promise you won't regret it.' And so I cut open my body and invited the parasite back in. Silently gnawing away at me from inside, he went unnoticed for several months until he invited me to a company barbeque that he was hosting. 'Have a beer with me, Max,' he asked with a clumsy and unwelcome familiarity. 'I just wanted to thank you again for giving me another shot, I truly appreciate it.' The beer tasted like cyanide. I choked it down as this parasite laughed at me from inside. He introduced me to his daughter and explained that she was to be starting university in Alberta come September. And now I see that they had begun breeding! This particular female offspring was well-endowed in her chest and hips, no doubt the result of many fine meals provided vicariously by me. She too had been allowed to thrive on my valuable innards. She was a part of me. She was made from me. She was mine. I take only partial credit for the events that followed as the signs were not particularly subtle. In her eyes I could see this creature's simple gears spinning. I had her not twenty minutes later in her basement bedroom after we stealthily stole away from the languid festivities. It was a trivial and conventional lay, though not an unimportant one. It was symbolic of me reclaiming what was mine and reuniting with my stolen flesh. She had told her father about our dalliance after a fight they had some weeks later. She wanted to hurt him. Parasitical cannibalism. He then confronted me about this, trying to strike a pathetic balance between anger and respect. The result of his inquiries? I fired him on the spot. The rage in his eyes suggested that he desired to attack me. Fortunately, this now starving creature had foresight enough to realize that such a decision would have resulted in his body becoming as thoroughly broken as his spirit now surely was. I had his daughter. I had stolen his career from him. And all he could think to do was slink away slowly, never to be heard from again, while I was made anew and left to feel pure and complete once more."

I stand mute, waiting for an out that eventually comes.

"I no longer retain any tolerance for parasites. Understand?"

I nod diligently.

"Then you'd best get to doing some writing."

## 21

# PROSOPOPOEIA

I OCCASIONALLY EXPERIENCE exploding head syndrome. It's a real thing, you can look it up if you don't believe me. Apparently it tends to be more common in women and in people over the age of fifty. It doesn't happen often, but when it does it will always be right as I'm about to fall asleep. Alarming to be sure, but as I understand it, not a cause for major concern. Now compared to that other thing that sometimes happens as I'm falling asleep, a bit of exploding head is a blessing in brevity.

You are aware of your surroundings, but you are unable to move, speak, or react in any way. This alone is a disturbing sensation, but one that is further compounded when you realize that your senses are caught skirting the line between the empirical and the subconscious. The dark denizens of your nightmares introduce themselves and you are incapable of reaction or evasion. When your personalized demons make their slow advance you regain the appreciation that you ought to have for the taken-for-granted gifts of mobility and speech. If you are strong, persistent, and blessed with a touch of good fortune, you may be able to jerk yourself awake before the icy hands of your unwelcome visitors reach out to caress you, but if your body remains lame and your chest stilled under unseen irons, you'll have no choice but to endure the advances while only bearing silent witness. This is how I have come to know fear in its most absolute and pure. No screen to look away from, no light to turn on, no safe word to hysterically utter. Just an inescapable embrace with your inner terror. You wake up to a barrage of cogitations and physical reactions not easily shaken off. Rapid palpitations, a heavy chest glazed in sweat, a slight sense of relief, but with a fearful respect of the darkness dormant within you. And always, the hope that such thing will never happen again.

Since beginning my residency as Montblanc's ghostwriter I have slept quite soundly despite the strangeness of the whole situation. I attribute this partially to the bed in the guestroom that I can only describe as 'immersive'. The rich just have a lot of things better than we do. One night on that bed can attest to this. Quite soundly, yes, until last night.

I had gone to sleep feeling anxious, something I try to avoid whenever possible, but I had been having doubts. M seemed largely unimpressed with my progress and product thus far and I was beginning to wonder whether I could write his book to the quality that he expected. Maybe he would fire me? The fragility of my ego under the stage lights. Maybe I would lose the money he promised that I so desperately wanted? Desperately needed? No, better make the distinction, we'll go with wanted. There needs to be a shred of something endearing about me. As I pondered my future and merit I slipped beyond the waking world to the peace of sleep, only to be interrupted by the unsettling feeling of paralysis. Try to move an arm. Try to roll over. Futility knows me tonight. I began to prepare my mental defences for the hellacious manifestations that I was expecting to see, but to my surprise my visitors did not seem to be of the macabre or otherworldly variety, rather, it was two men. Familiar men. Men that I had known since my youth. Men whose voices were burned into memories I hadn't yet discovered.

The first man looked rather svelte, though this may have been an illusion caused by his well-fitting suit, complete with a white shirt and navy blue tie. His hair was graying and thinning and he struck me as a healthy, honest, and hard-working figure. The second man, seemingly older than his companion as evidenced by his snow-white goatee and seasoned blue eyes, was wearing a jacket with a black-and-white checkerboard design. A hideous jacket by any account, but he did not seem a man concerned with the opinions of others. The duo looked over me for a moment before they began conversing, though for reasons unclear at the time it took me far longer than it should have to

realize that they were speaking about me. The older, more bois-
terous and garrulous of the two opened the discussion.

"Get a load of this slacker here! All you kids out there listen
up and watch closely—you can't be doing this kind of stuff if you
want to compete at this level. What happened in the old days, if
you were caught slackin' like this, the coach wouldn't pull you
aside like they do today, he'd call you out in front of the whole
team and you better believe that drove the message home!"

"You think it might have something to do with the schedule
that many of these guys are on? They—"

"Nah, don't give me any of that, these young guys are pampered today as far as I'm concerned. And look what happens! First
of all, with the way they come up nowadays they aren't made
accountable for their mistakes. You pamper these guys and they
get soft and lazy and they aren't held accountable. This is supposed
to be the toughest game in the world, but when you get these
pampered young guys with their West Coast attitude—"

"Now hold on, Grapes, some of your favourite players are
West Coasters, I don't think that's—"

"Never mind that, those boys you're talkin' about played
most their lives in Ontario learning how to play the game right.
Give me a good Kitchener boy over these West Coasters any day
of the week. Anyhow, watch this guy here—here's what you
can't be doing, kids. You got to show a little passion. I tell ya, if
these guys played with any of the intensity that Bobby played
with they wouldn't be in this position. I don't care how much
talent you have, without the intensity it's gonna be wasted every
time!"

"What about this one, you think he'll be able to bounce
back?"

"Ah, he's a good kid, just needs to smarten up. I'll tell ya
something from my coaching days—we had this one young guy,
small guy, not much more than five and a half feet, but what a
player. He knew he was never gonna be a big guy, but lemme
tell ya, he went out there every night he and played like he was
the biggest guy on the ice, and boy were the other teams scared
of him! One of the toughest guys I ever known and it just goes

to show ya that the fire inside is worth more than anything else. And you know what folks? This guy here's got some fire in him yet, believe it! He's gonna be a beauty!"

## 22

## PALIMPSEST

WHO ARE YOU, Abigail Edington, and what role might you fulfill on this intrepid journey of ours? I might have lived my entire life without noticing the breadcrumbs of your own. Were it my fate to craft we would share our discoveries under dead or dying stars as black-clad choirmen sing in a language I would only pretend to understand. Alas, all I have is your digital footprint, fumbled upon during my perfunctory pursuit of prosaic perfection, and from this I know that Montblanc's history can wait. I don't know how great nor simple minds operate, but I will know no peace of mine until I pursue this unannounced question with the diligence it is due—who are you Abigail Edington? On the 24th of April 2015, an answer is attempted in the form of a post from your sparsely-coloured, templated landing page:

> *My name is Abigail Edington and I was born in the year*
> *2000. I am a photographer, graphic designer, writer, and*
> *Reformed Christian, and I am writing my first novel! This blog*
> *is a place for me to share my writing and my pictures and just*
> *my general overall thoughts on things. I hope you enjoy!*
> *With love,*
> *Abby*

A dozen sugar-coated strawberries for this Child of God, fifteen years young and somehow between the Sunday singing of hymns in her modest floral dress and the predicted pitfalls prescribed to her cohort she finds time enough not only to undertake the writing of a novel but also to maintain a blog dedicated to the specificities of the undertaking itself. And at twice her age what have I to offer but my own shallow meditation on the process? But this isn't about me—who are you, Abigail Edington? I scroll down her landing page, blue text on white background, and open the post entitled 'Choosing a Pen Name', dated April 27th, 2015:

*My name isn't really Abigail Edington. I keep my real name a secret for privacy reasons, but also because I wanted my pen name to be something unique. I chose the name Abigail because it means "the Father's joy" in Hebrew and because Abigail was the name of King David's wife. The Bible describes Abigail as intelligent and beautiful. Not like I see myself that way or anything, but I figured my pen name should portray confidence. I also just think it's a really pretty name. Choosing a pen name can be hard, it took a long time to narrow mine down to something that I liked and that sounded good when I said it out loud. I still feel like it would be really weird and hard to get used to being called something other than my real name if my novel ever got published and famous but the more I write it and say it the more natural it sounds. It would be so crazy to see it in print one day!*
*With love,*
*Abby*

A penname, is it? Not something I have ever considered for myself. I quite like the exotic flair inherent in 'Larry Mann.' Sounds like the name of a plumber. I suppose I could just go with L. S. Mann, or maybe by my middle name—Sierra Mann. I never did forgive my parents for that one. I need more clues Abigail. What else do you have for me? On the inspirational power of music, May 5th, 2015:

*I like to listen to music when I write, especially instrumental music. It's fascinating how the melodies of instruments can bring out feelings of sadness, happiness, and nostalgia. I find that the emotions that music makes me feel really help with my writing, especially when I need to capture the relationship between two characters. In my novel there are many different*

*types of relationships between all the characters and some of*
*these have very established musical soundtracks in my head.*
*I've put together a playlist of some of my favourite instrumental*
*songs. Maybe they can bring out the same emotions in you that*
*they brought out in me!*
*With love,*
*Abby*

Damn, girl, your novel has more than two characters? I feel
like I am getting closer to knowing who you are, but as I tem-
porize my way through the entirety of the content on Abigail's
blog I notice the pattern of her updates. She posted consistently
and excitingly for about two months, and then, nothing. Not a
single update since the early summer of 2015 nearly three years
ago. And now? The blog is a ghost town, preserving the archi-
tecture of a precocious and idealistic young artist in a buried corner of the Internet that no one will likely ever see again. But
what ever became of the young Abigail? Did she finish her book?
Does she still write at all? In desperation I try searching her pen
name for any signs of recent activity but I find nothing. Nothing.
And suddenly I feel betrayed and alone. Had she strayed from the
path like so many others have? From the path that I still doggedly
walk despite the incessant harassment of my better judgement?
One by one I've seen my peers come to their senses and free
themselves. I see guitars locked in their cases collecting dust. I see
dancing shoes tucked away in boxes at the bottoms of closets. I
see wooden hockey sticks standing guard in garages. And where
is the young Abigail now? Waiting tables at some overpriced
chain restaurant that forces her into tight black clothing that further constricts her will to creation?

I'm sorry Abigail Edington. With purity of intent I
wanted to tell them who you were, but all I found on the screen
was a glimpse of my own visage reflected against your white
background. All we can be is ourselves and all we can have is
each other.

With love,
L. Sierra Mann

## 23

## PALINGENESIS

AN UNUSUALLY LATE dinner tonight as Monsieur Montblanc returns from a brief trip to Ottawa. Unusually late and unusually silent. I had already eaten about four hours prior, but at the Big Man's insistence I joined him at the dining room table. As if there were any real choice in the matter. By now I had accepted that my tenure as his ghostwriter came with other obligations, some-thing I had to remind myself of as I sat at across from him in my sleepwear watching him eat in silence. Still, it felt odd that despite his apparent desire for my company he had not yet spoken any weighed words or near any at all. I have absolute confidence in my ability to win this little game of taciturnity, but I feel an empathetic poltergeist tugging on my tongue. He wants to say something. I can tell. I would know that feeling a dozen bodies away. In a flash of a moment, a single-frame of blinking light, I feel sympathy for the mum and monumental man sitting across the table, as if I have the power to somehow help him. As if I am supposed to. Sympathy for the man who has more than me in every respect. In an act that I immodestly felt transcended the trappings of internal confliction, I make a meager attempt to open a dialogue.

"How-how-how wuh-wuh-was Ot-Ottawa?"

"As it happens my appetite is not as mighty as I felt it to be. Come now, show me what you have written today if you would."

I excuse myself, leave the table, and head to the office down-stairs where I print the chapter I had been working on that day. I return to the table, now cleared, and hand Montblanc a few pages like a cat delivering a dead bird. Without hesitation, he begins reading aloud and I immediately wish that he hadn't. Forced now to face the discomfort of hearing my own words recited back to me I become hyperaware to any examples of bad grammar or awkward wording.

"I had walked up the steps of Parliament Hill several times before, but in December of 2000 I walked up them for the first time as a Member of Parliament."

He stops dictating, but his eyes are still darting from one side of the page of the other as I watch for any break in his stoic expression.

"So it is to be a series of moments is it?"

An inquisitive look on my face as he starts again.

"Why are you in front of me in those rags? Could you not be bothered to get dressed? You are in a dangerous position, you do realize that, yes?"

"You, you, you want me to . . . to . . . to get d-d-d-d-dressed?"

"Do not let your ignorance shine through, Laurent. You are before me in rags, offering me a series of moments, a series of my own moments. I will ask you again and you had best answer plain—do you realize that you are in a dangerous position?"

"A d-d-d-d-d-dangerous puh-puh-puh-puh—"

"*Tabernac*, out with it already! I've never before met a man who claims himself a wordsmith yet butchers the language so egregiously. Is that all you are capable of? Parroting my words back to me as a fractured mess in the form of a question? Do not do me that disservice. Do not do yourself that disservice. If you can only speak one language you had best learn to speak it properly. Now answer the bloody question."

"I-I-I-I don't know wuh-wuh-wuh—"

"Get up. Now. Follow me."

Max leaves the table and leads me back downstairs to the office.

"Sit down."

He points to the chair at the desk and I oblige.

"Now write."

He stands behind me and points to the computer. I shrug my shoulders and turn both palms upwards.

"It's to be a series of moments, is it? So write about a moment from your own life and do not think about stopping until you have finished."

I stare at the screen, avoiding the possibility of eye contact. I think he sees my hands shaking. His voice slightly softens.

"Listen. I know there are things you would say to me right now, and I know that you cannot. You know that you cannot. There lives a demon in your throat that slices up every word that passes though, but he wields no influence in your mind. Never mind the blood or the muscles, I want you to write and I don't want you to stop. Write with no fear. Transcend your broken flesh. Lay your soul bare and conqueror what pain so ails you. You wear rags now, but you will write like a king. Paint me a moment if that is indeed what you are so inclined to do. Go. Now."

In chaos and confusion, I create a new document and set my hands on the keyboard.

"Don't dwell, just write."

And so I did.

*I had hiked up the mountain by the river several times before, but in December of 2003 I hiked up it with a specific purpose in mind. I wanted to get away, much like I do right now. I wanted to find a place where no one could find me so that I could do at the time what I felt needed to be done. I woke up early that morning and set off without telling anybody. It was snowing lightly and still dark outside. As I made toward the river I passed through the industrial district and in one of the yards I saw an automated cage used to capture bears. I fantasized about encountering a bear on my way up the mountain and I thought about all the things that it could do to me. Every scenario I envisioned ended with me being maimed and painted red atop the fresh snow. I felt content in this possibility. It would be a good way to go. And what would they all say about me? Would they feel bad? I hoped that they would be forced to hear all of the graphic details. My only wish would be to see it myself.*

*Soon after I made it to the river. While I knew there was a bridge a half kilometre away, at one point I saw that there was just enough ice formed on the riverbank to form a jumpable gap. I tested the integrity of the ice a few times before I nervously but successfully leaped the distance. I was at the foot of the mountain now, but still nowhere near the trails. I didn't want to be anywhere near them. I started hiking straight up. Slippery and steep, the ascent was a physically difficult one. As my legs turned to fire the thought of my eventual reward propelled me forward. One grueling step after another, I knew the summit would eventually come, and with it, my release.*

I stop typing just long enough for M to remind me of his presence.

"Don't stop, keep going."

And I do, but the tense changes and sways and it's hard to keep track. It was then too.

*Under laboured breath, stiff muscles, and my own unwavering determination I soon reached the clearing at the top—that place where I knew I wouldn't be found. It was early in the afternoon now and the sunlight was causing the snow around me to sparkle. It looked like the snow was weeping. It was almost too bright to look at. I made it. The last challenge was over. I took out the notepad and the pen from my back pocket and began writing the proclamation that I knew I needed to write at the time. And then I sat. I sat in the snow, looking toward the sun with the entire town in view. I don't know how long I sat there, but I remember feeling blessed and thankful for what was before me. I don't know if it was the elevation, or the view, or some divine or spiritual intervention, but I felt each breath deeper than ever, as if I were drawing in more oxygen than I ever had before. When the time felt right, I stood up to begin my descent. I took one small detour to peer over an edge overlooking the river, and as I did, the ground beneath me broke and I fell, tumbling down the cliff and toward the angry river below. There was nothing to grab onto during the fall. All I could do was prepare for my landing in the water. I felt the frigidity before I felt the pain. Heightened adrenaline acts as a natural painkiller. The river pulled me as I felt the rocks on my legs, blunt and unforgiving. It will be over soon. Just go to sleep.*

*I was found shortly after on the side of the river by an elderly man walking his dog. I still remember seeing the orange stripes of his tracksuit as I came to, cold, bruised, and bloodied.*

*And soon came the whispers.*

*"Why else would he go up there by himself without telling any-one?"*

*"He's always had a hard time making friends in school, you know."*

*"He's very reserved because of his impediment."*

*I told everyone from the doctors, to my parents, to the other kids at school that I was just there to hike, but deep down I knew that none of them believed that. Everything was different after that, and not in the way that I had originally intended. During the fall my only exonerating evidence, the notepad, fell out of my pocket and was presumably carried down the river toward the Pacific.*

I stop writing again, but instead of an order I get a question.

"What was it that you wrote on that notepad?"

I close the document. 'Do you want to save changes to Document 1?' No. I turn around and make eye contact with Maxime for the first time since we left the dinner table. I stay silent and a quarter-smile forms on his face.

"Point taken."

He rests his hand on my shoulder.

"Goodnight, Lawrence."

He leaves the room and I stay seated for awhile staring at a white computer screen that now resembles snow.

Point taken.

## 24

## Petulance

I AM SPEAKING directly now to Leonard Cohen, the Amethyst Jew. What is Montblanc's position on that trouble over in Israel?

Float me some words. I feel dry in my knees, my bare bones breathing brittle wisps of limited oxygen. I was once gravel stuck to your sandals, walking with you across the beaches of Hydra. I'm here now as your forgotten son, asking for the overdue alimony I am owed. Please pops! Toss one back with your bastard. I've wrested and I've weened between the unclean and the serene, the obscene scenes seen leaking through your wrinkled seams. I've scanned the environs both immediate and intangible for a sign that I've done all that which I've endeavored to do. Anxiously I check the mail every day at half after eleven for the telegram I know will never come.

LAWRENCE SIERRA MANN <STOP> WITH THE COLLECTIVE VOICE OF THE ENTIRE NATION WE WOULD LIKE TO THANK YOU FOR YOUR UNWAVERING CANDOUR AND UNBREAK-ABLE WILL <STOP> FORGIVE THE LATENESS OF THIS COMMENDATION <STOP> LITTLE IS AS LITTLE DOES <STOP> WE LOVE YOU <STOP> WE ALWAYS WILL <STOP> <FULL STOP>

Still—nary enough, never was. And it won't be until I earn your good graces. The critics are fickle; they say my sentence structures are all the same. No variety. Tired and obvious metaphors. Needlessly opaque. These slanders I can forgive, but only so long as I am able to find acceptance in your eyes.

I never wanted to walk on the moon, I would have sent my son instead. A strong support network provided by my unscarred and underworked hands. To the stars my dear boy, and never shall you need to worry about securing the love of your father. Do you see now the clarity of my perils? Rushing red firetrucks stop in front of the nursery, the first responders look younger every year. I see them on their nights off, inside the grocery store, dallying about the eighth aisle with their ladies—securing the night's provisions. All matter is subject to change. Do you accept this statement? If you do, then perhaps it is not too late for us to stage a reconciliation under the public gaze? 628 loons carrying us across the pond, upwards toward the heights you were kind enough to visit from. Your wet gunpowder isn't helping. In meditation you witness craven images of subordinate lilies and a garden soon overgrown. I want to be pure in your eyes. Deem me worthy of inheriting your infinite ink bottle.

I don't count myself amongst the ignoble rabble who would fuck to save their species but wouldn't run to save their lives. But then, who would? Ask me if there is reason in my responses, ask anyone, and affirmation will become familiar to you. So where doth such incessant incredulity make berth? I am not yet a registered sperm donor, but I've been thinking about it more frequently. My demand is that whatever product results from my frozen fellas be introduced to me in its best attire at the age of twenty-five. Let them see firsthand that their daddy does indeed maintain a corporeal form. I willingly offer them that courtesy, so why can't you?

I am speaking directly now to Leonard Cohen, the Amethyst Jew. Can you hear me? Give me something. Give me anything. My feet are soon to meet the ocean floor.

## 25

## PARSIMONY

"SHORT CHAPTERS, LARRY. That's the way to go about it. Our current media climate thrives on succinct encapsulations of ideas and feelings and so too shall we. Write for the rushed, do not spare a single wasted word. Is this agreeable to you?"

"Sure thing, M-Mmmax."

"Very good, although truth be told I expected more resistance to this idea. Are you not a self-professed student of speech-craft and wordsmithery? Are you not one who enjoys discharging his verbosity all over the page after a heated round of loquacious self-pleasure? Will you find it difficult to refrain from masturbating within the paragraphs of my chronicles?"

"I'll muh-mmm-manage."

"You'll manage . . . Oh, mild-mannered Larry. Were this conversation to take place on a battlefield where you might stand on both legs I wonder if your subservience would give way to more formidable responses. It's uncommon that I meet someone of high enough caliber worth verbally sparring with, I'll ask that you not squander this opportunity for me. Still, we meet on this plane unevenly matched and must find a way to circumvent your handicap. What say you to a game of *Scrabble?*"

Not exactly what I was expecting, but given that this is one of the more normal requests Monty has made recently, I'm willing to oblige. Besides, having spent the finer moments of my youth with my mouth shut and my nose buried in the dictionary, *Scrabble* is a game I've some proficiency with. I agree to his challenge, and I see a child-like glee in his eyes as he darts up from the dining room table to retrieve the game from the nearby room. He continues speaking as he leaves the room, the resonance of his voice slightly diminished.

"I know you have interpreted your impediment as something of a curse, and rightly so I should think, still, believe me when I say that the alternative is not without its own set of inconveniences. A man in my position is not allowed to waste words, nor is he meant to publicly engage in any intriguing arrangements of them. Earlier in my political life I used to write my own speeches, but that is an agency I have since had to relinquish."

He returns and places the *Scrabble* box on the table. It's an older version of the game—it looks just like the copy they had at my old elementary school. The box is covered in a thin layer of dust, a fact that along with Montblanc's apparent giddiness to play suggests that it hasn't been opened in quite some time.

"Words are surgical tools. A banal story told with the right combination of words can become entrancing. This is an art my current speechwriters have perfected. They know the precise amount of words that can be properly digested by the general public and in what order they are most palatably delivered. I must admit their skills are quite commendable. Did you ever read *Moby-Dick*? Its admirers will point out that it contains over 200,000 words of beautiful symbolism and prose, while its critics will point out the exact same thing. One star in the sky is a marvelous sight, itself an isolated miracle, but what does that one star lose when positioned among the galaxy's innumerable? Take my point? Short chapters. That's what my book needs. Obtuse wordiness will not be met well."

I force a contemplative look onto my face in an attempt to convince Max that I am pondering and processing his words, when in actuality my mind is focused on the wooden *Scrabble* tile now held between my thumb and index finger. I recognize the wood as maple. The wondrous wood of this land and all others north of the line—invisible to those standing on the location etched onto the globes made in sunken, overheated factories. The leaf of this proud genus adorning the national flag and stirring within me a patriotism, artificially indoctrinated through the

lessons learned while sat at an ill-fitted desk made of the same
special wood. I recall now my own, found in the third parallel
row of six, fifth position of five. A knot of the wood still visible
on the surface, smoothly sanded and with an assembly line veneer
applied. During unimaginative lessons of rudimentary algebra, I
would fixate on the knot, itself the size of a Canadian two-dollar
coin, which is known colloquially as the 'toonie', and is the
largest standard coin found in the Canadian currency. The toonie
was introduced as legal tender in the year 1996. The coin is
unique in that its outer circumference is both ridged and smooth,
alternating between the two terrains. However, while the toonie
is perfectly round, the knot on my desk, though similar in size,
was not of similar geographic soundness. It was instead a random
and disjointed shape, unpleasing to an eye that has been trained
to search for perpendicularity and rule. Though a markedly different look from the rest of the manufactured maple, if one
closed their eyes and ran their fingers across the knot, they would
notice no difference in touch. What I've learned of senses,
betrayed by the incompatibility between sight and touch, and I
am left to meander on the role that knots play in the lifecycle of
their towering hosts. In the lifespan of a standard maple, which
can last hundreds of years, several branches are grown, many of
which outlive their usefulness and will ultimately drop off from
the trunk leaving behind an imperfect reminder that will eventually become a knot. This is why many of them have a relatively
circular shape as opposed to more chaotic arrangements. Knots
are not found and created arbitrarily, they are the physical scars
of outgrown wooden limbs. Watchers of these limbs and of the
forest floors on which they land have known several names
including *Nemestrinus*, *Porewit*, *Medeina*, and *Tapio*, and are often
depicted as valiant hunters, so it is easy to overlook their contri-
butions to the creation of the knot on my desk in lieu of this
more daring imagery. I would caution against adopting a glam-
orized interpretation of the forest deities and their workings, and
will point to the example of Arthur Froley to illustrate the importance of this warning. In the seventeenth century, Arthur Froley,
sworn to the throne of Charles I, walked the woods of present

day Vermont, and while officially employed as a trader, he additionally practiced in the arts of cartography and dendrology, finding himself fascinated with the forests and landscapes of the New World. Noticing the similarities between the maples of his homeland and those of these foreign forests, Arthur Froley concluded, with a conviction characteristic of the time, that the trees must have been placed by a divine force, the subtle differences between them simply a matter of the different air and fauna found on this new continent. As he sat under a particularly mighty maple, sketching the dense view in front of him, Arthur Froley was struck on the head by a falling branch that was a moment previous attached to the very tree his back was resting against. The strike of the branch, itself the size of a mature man's thigh, did not immediately kill Arthur Froley, though it did render him unconscious. That night he would freeze to death, while a fresh knot on the murderous maple was formed. Prior to his demise, Arthur Froley had frequently envisioned returning to England as a hero and being personally commended by King Charles himself. Thoughts of this ceremony and the indulgent feast that would follow provided existential nourishment for Arthur Froley during the cold and lonely winters he spent away from country and family. He had pictured the royal hall and the seemingly limitless variety of dishes that were to be served within it, prepared and garnished by the most talented chefs in the entire kingdom. The meats that would be separated effortlessly from bone, the thick soups with their chemically pure combination of spices, and the wines, O Heavens—the wines! The royal vineyards persevering through the glassy heart of December to fulfill their promise of delivery. And with abundant choices, by the by. Sparkling wine, having only recently been invented when product from Champagne underwent secondary fermentation during winter storage. While this bubbling variety was considered by the French to be treason against the Lords of Drink, it was well-received on the tongues of the English, and presumably, would have been by Arthur Froley as well. Alas, by the machinations of some fate, Arthur Froley's throat was to remain perpetually unintroduced to the bubbles of his distant home, while his maps, crude as they may have been, were lost to the mighty winds of Vermont. The remains of his body were likely stripped of all valuables by the resident Iroquois before becoming food for the various woodland creatures inhabiting the area. On the subject of the woodland's fauna, while human remains were not an expected part of their daily diets, the arrival of European explorers did alter the ecosystems in many ways, some implications of which still linger today. For example . . .

Wait. Hold on a minute. What was Monty talking about? Something about not wasting words and keeping things brief? That shouldn't be too hard. As he finishes preparing the game board I return the letter tile I was holding to the bag and blindly grab seven others.

D S U I R T N.

Rust? Dust? Runt? Sun? Not much to go with here. As I contemplate whether or not 'TURDS' is an acceptable word to play, my opponent begins the game, placing the word 'HASTY', the 'H' on the center star, the 'Y' now resting on a double letter tile.

"For thirty points."

"G-g-g-ood start," I hesitantly admit, my stutter here the result of nervousness as opposed to whatever it is normally the result of. Maybe it was the word that Max just placed subconsciously urging me to hurry, or maybe it was my own arrogant desire to show him how quickly I can play this silly game, but I made my move almost instantly after he made his. I play the word 'DUSTY' using his freshly laid 'Y' tile as my anchor.

"Eighteen."

As Montblanc begins to mark my score I realize the result of my hasty and under-calculated move. Maybe you have too? I could have played the word 'INDUSTRY' and cleared my whole row to the tune of seventy-four points. I briefly consider asking Montblanc if I can make a revision, but I decide not to. And just like that the stakes of this game became plain to me— this isn't a friendly match or a superfluous contest. No, I'm playing this game for the sanctity of my soul—a wager I put up without even realizing. Maximus the Manipulator has goaded me into defending myself against his smiling inquiries into my own redundancy, and by the end of the first turn I've already surrounded my pole position. Let me pose a question—if Max can beat me at this game, why does he need me around at all? Let's review. I've dropped what could have been a forty-four-point lead, left now to climb back from a twelve-point deficit. These little maple tiles don't represent letters of the alphabet and their corresponding point values, they represent a domain that I am expected to have a certain degree of mastery over.

My opponent, who seems to have inexplicably grown in size, plays the word 'STUMP', using the 'U' that I placed during my premature opening turn.

"For eighteen."

Fuck you. I know how many points the word is worth you prick. You think I'm too stupid to add up a few small numbers? Why would you play that word anyway? Are you trying to intimidate me or something? To 'stump' me? Typical politician. Double-dealing knaves, the whole lot of them. I nod my head, chocking back the urge to flip the board off the table.

"Tell me, Larry, when did you first discover your affinity for the written word?"

The hell kind of question is that? Is he trying to thrown me off? Wait, is he being sarcastic? It's goddamn *Scrabble,* did he expect me to recreate *Sonnet 18* on the board? The letters you get are random you lack-linen mate! I'm seething now. It has been suggested that I tend to take these things a little too seriously, but this time I believe I am justified. I'm on course to lose this game. And then what? 'Sorry, Larry, I guess you just weren't the penman I thought you were, maybe I'd best get someone else to finish my book.' And there I go, back to B.C. with my tail between my legs. Back to my mattress in the corner of my room. Back to the ever-open gates of oblivion. Forget that. Forget the game. I need to appeal directly to whatever humanity still exists within Mister Meal Ticket. Deep breath, elongate the words if you need to, just no stuttering, this has to be pure.

"I can wrrrrrite your book."

"Yes, I know, that's why you are here. Still, I'm curious as to how your creative genesis occurred. Was it simply a matter of being in the company of books at an early age?"

He's looking at me. He's having a conversation with me. You see, when two people are engaged in a conversation, they tend to look at each other. What he's not looking at is the game board. He's not looking at his letters, in fact, I think he forgot to replenish his tile supply after playing his last word. And just like that the realization slaps me across the face—he doesn't give a damn about the outcome of the game, he's just happy to be able to play it with someone. With someone who isn't on his official staff. With someone who isn't expected to engage in relentless acts of sycophantism. With someone he can have a conversation with. A conversation that's not on the record. A conversation that won't have political repercussions. A conversation with someone that he, for whatever reason, seems to trust. A conversation with me, speech impediment and all. For one flash of a moment my mind dwells on how utterly unlikeable I feel myself to be at times before starkly shifting toward the prevailing irony that surrounds us.

This chapter, which opens with Montblanc outlining the importance of short chapters, is in fact one of the longest chapters in the book.

Wait, what book?

Oh Lord, it's happening again . . .

## 26

## PORTENTOUSNESS

MIRED IN THE bramble now, sleeping two floors under a man like I was his pet Jojo. Treat me like a Fabergé egg and handle me with your surgical gloves. There's nothing to be said here that's worth saying. A book about a writing man writing a book about a man written by a writing man who writes books about writing men. Any writer who writes a book where the main character is a writer is a hack and that's a fact.

The air is dangerously thin at the top, my friends, but trust that I have noticed the uneasy footing on each of the broken bodies I've ungraciously doddered over. Here's one: disingenuousness is bubbling over the side of the pot. It makes a right horrid mess. The ordeal panics me and in my haste I knock over the whole damn thing. Visions of the glossy pages of office supply catalogues and my duty as an informed and disciplined consumer to select the paper shredder that is right for me. Burn it all to the ground. Kerosene. Ethanol. Frustration begets anger, anger arms the hackneyed legions that insist on calling me 'brother.'

The first word on today's practice list is 'property.' The 'p' words are always tough to begin with, but this one comes with additional challenges. It goes from one hard 'p' sound to another with little room between them. Even if I can make it past the first one I can't waste a moment to celebrate before the spotlight shines on the next. If I'm still standing after that one-two combo, the 't' at the end will try its best to finish the bout.

Be great at the things you are capable of being great at. I thought I knew what those things were. In grade school I was a pretty good distance runner. I abandoned it when the training started becoming too difficult. I remember seeing my former coach a few months later at the grocery store and feeling what was at the time an unfamiliar sensation. It's been felt often enough since.

Puhrrrroprty. Not bad. We can do better though. We can. We could. We might.

Maybe the difference between me and those who look like me lies in my capacity for acts of extreme bravery. &&*^&((^^!. Something for the cryptographers. But the rest of them? They would never do that kind of shit. Mark it, friends, this will be something special.

No, no, that doesn't work either. The threads of my disguise are unravelling. But wait! Maybe this inside look endears me? No? Well, it was worth a shot. The problem is that I haven't any idea what you want. Problem? That's a good one, let's make that the next practice word.

I had a friend in high-school who fancied herself an artist. How I loathed that label and my implied association with it! She specialized in drawing skulls with varying degrees of ornateness, but she ultimately failed to develop in her craft. We march now side-by-side, though one day I dream of escaping these synchronized steps and returning to the sea's expanse. Returning to the longship where I can sit and row anonymously with my Viking brethren. On every third stroke I like to fake it. I haven't yet been caught.

Alright. Enough is enough. I currently have one singular purpose—to write the memoirs of Maxime Montblanc. He's sleeping two floors above me now. Sometimes I feel like his pet Jojo. But that's it. That's what I am. I'm an employee. An errand boy. One in my position would certainly benefit from letting go of these delusions of artistry and mockery.

## 27

# PARAMOUR

"THERE REMAINS NOTHING unique left to be said on the topic of love, wouldn't you agree, Lawrence?"

"I've never-never-never tuh-trrrr-tried."

"No, I never expected you to trespass such quotidian grounds. Though I wonder of the folly inherent in your decision."

"How do you, how do you muh-muh . . . mmm-mean?"

"There are but a select few matters in this world that so universally flow through us and pump blood through the heart of the human condition. Banal mayhap to you or I, but necessities all the same. Now surely I cannot be expected to omit the role that love has played in my life's story. My suggestion—I recommend you include only the barest of essentials. I met my wife, we married, and we remain so to this day. I insist that you keep any coverage of my official romantic history as stylistically inelegant as possible, no need for any ostentatious displays. What the people need to know is that I love my wife and that I have successfully maintained the institution of marriage. For what man is fit to reign who cannot hold firm those of his own life? Authenticity and consistency are good enough for them. No need to bleed into scrupulous displays of over-emotion, nothing has been proven to stir contempt so furiously. Weakness come alive. Here we must walk the line with no desire to draw our own. *D'accord*?"

"Sounds g-g-g-g-good."

"Very good, however, with this now established I do have a thought beyond this agreement that I would like to share if you would permit me. I will caution you that it addresses what you may consider the tired topic of love in a way that you might find unexpected, though it is a thought that has been weighing heavier on me with each passing year. A thought I have not uttered or exposed to anyone. You surely see that there is an implication of trust in my desire to share it with you. Knowing this, will you allow me to continue?"

"Yes, puh-puh-please do, Muh-Mmmm-Max."

"My dear accomplice. You have been made privy to my many sins of flesh. You know I have philandered and engaged in a great number of casual dalliances ranging in their perversity. You know my marriage is but a Potemkin village hiding a hollowed husk inside. You know I have little concern to follow the edicts of companionship, my success in life due to a romantic celibacy of sorts. What you know is truth, though a truth incomplete.

"I had known him from the age of twenty-two, blossoming then in the art of interpretation and as a student of sensation, yet to be numbed, yet to be a closed bracket at the end of the page. In his eyes, always unmoved, unsettlingly focused—one of his many skills I would come to adopt—I saw reflection. A comradery of similarities from the profane to the profound. Our story was written with an uncharacteristic haste, curiously devoid of grammatical error and with an unspoken confidence. It was about four years later when I started to digest some of the feelings trepidatiously traipsing around the recesses of my mind. Cavernous icicles melting, drop by drop. In fact, I can place this far more accurately to a precise square on the calendar and specific coordinates on the globe. Enter an odyssey of us, planned in advance for a day when any and all earthly obligations were distant points on the horizon.

"And on that glorious day we knew each other as we knew ourselves. Intimate, exposed, and safely cherished above all. We were the denizens of the Great Mother's opulence. We were the dirty-footed nomads, graciously stumbling through our dance of elation and psilocybin. We were the caretakers of each other's concerns, transposed to flat stone and skipped across the water to the eternal rest of the lakebed beneath. Moving seamlessly from one moment of tranquility to the next I caught myself flirting with a path I have known to be dangerous in situations as these. An uninvited thought asking why I had to leave this behind. Why must I awake to the shrill alarms of expectation not of my own definition? What justice is it that I cannot feel like this always? Insomuch that a moment or experience can beg these unanswerable questions, I was quick to acknowledge that my longing for peace was nothing more than a powerful longing to remain in his company. To feel the absence of judgement and the assurance that my words were not just heard, but felt. Does this arouse such excitement as to remain unobtainable? The Christmas mornings of my youth calling to me from the past, a lost time when the overabundance of agency had not yet been introduced.

"But you know the answers to these questions. You know where I am today, in front of you and dwelling on a story that has no sequel. Only recently can I fully admit this, but I have never felt that way about another person before. Whether that makes it love or simply the unfulfilled longing for a sun that had to set, never to be seen again—on that I do not know. Nor do I need to. We tend to construct visions of what could be that are impervious to the harsh conditions of reality. Maybe that is a comforting thought, though I can still occasionally hear his voice in my head. I can still feel him sitting beside me in my fleeting moments of existential dread, assuring me that these are indeed days worth conquering. If these memories, beautiful and forlorn as they are to me, have met you with any discomfort, I surely apologize, but I needed to mention them to someone. I needed to prove to myself that they existed, that they happened, that they touched me and that they shaped me. I have done terrible things to many people, but what humanity remains within me is unequivocally attributable to him. And how real it was."

"Wuh-wuh-when was the . . . last t-t-t-time . . . you spoke to him?"

"No, young Lawrence, not now. Not now or ever again I'm afraid. It's long past time I returned these concerns to the soft sand from which they formed—that I might sleep unhaunted once more."

# 28

## PALLIATION

MONTBLANC IS SLEEPING upstairs. If I were to strangle him in his sleep, the whole country would be forced to learn my name.

Nothing even happens in this book. Why are you still here?

# Pugilism

HAVE WE ANY magicians or spin doctors on retainer? The life of one Montblanc comma M proves to be a palette rich with colours not suitable for public consumption. I'm doing my best to cut around the bruises of this apple but what remains edible is disappearing fast. Under finicky angles and fortuitous lighting an attractive form flickers into frame, but too often these ideal circumstances evade us and I'm left with a charge well beyond my limited expertise. I'm no artist. At my best I'm a semi-competent scribe. I know what M wants, he's been clear about that. Gathering and presenting important dates and milestones in a coherent manner, that's easy. But portraying Montblanc as an endearing and inspiring figure? Well that might just be my Waterloo.

There's certainly no shortage of slanderous content written about the man. I could curate a three-volume philippic just with the anonymous comments left on various blogs and news sites. They say he's dangerous. They say he doesn't represent Canadian values. Some even say that he's evil. 'Evil', as if he were supervillain. But I know Max better than those people do. He's not evil. What does evil mean anyway? But a certain something does seem to emanate from him. I hesitate to call it a darkness, but it's something. Something beyond my own projections and interpretations. I submit to the jury last night's dinner conversation. After a lengthy lull in our conversation, which to this point had been trivial, the accused broke the silence.

"I can recall with uncompromised clarity the feeling of collapsing cartilage against my knuckles. I had entered puberty at a relatively early age and by thirteen I was markedly larger in stature than most of my peers, still a fact today. It was my size that was the focus of ridicule that day. James Colquhoun shared my age but attended a secularized public school that had been erected adjacent to a small forest that has long since been cut down. When he came across me in this forest he was with his brother, three years his senior and whose name was never uttered. All I knew of the family Colquhoun was what my mother would insipidly account to my father at the dinner table. Routinely she would share whispers and canards of neighbouring families to my father who by this point would scarcely feign any interest beyond a mechanical nodding of his head, his eyes ever focused on his plate. Pedestrian as my family dinners were, the Colquhoun boys would likely look upon them with envy. Their father had been in prison for the better part of five years following a violent streak that culminated in the near-murder of a fellow miner for reasons lost to rampant speculation. Apparently his violence had routinely found its way home to Mrs. Colquhoun, though she never once confirmed this. Despite my averted gaze and fast steps, the brothers Colquhoun were intent on engaging with me on my way through the woods. They wanted to know how big my mother's cunt was that I could be pushed out of it. It was the older brother who said this and it was him I chose to target. It was the first time I had been stirred to the point of violence and it occurred not because I felt an overwhelming need to protect the honour of my mother or what reputation I may have had, it occurred precisely because I did not want it to occur. After the first strike the elder Colquhoun fell to his back and I followed closely, landing on top of him. I can't say with certainty how many blows my barrage consisted of, but it was roughly a dozen before James through primal volition could separate the two of us. I drew rapid breaths as I looked down upon the mostly still body of the elder Colquhoun, his left eye involuntarily shut and his nose unnaturally displaced, pointing now to the side rather than straightaway. A prayer, for he was not an attractive man to begin with. Wordlessly I resumed my journey through the forest at a pace now even quicker than the one that failed to dissuade my agitator. As the adrenaline produced by the exchange began to fade and the pain in my hand hitherto unnoticed became more pronounced, I remember feeling sympathetic toward James, for it wasn't James who pitched insults, on the contrary, he was silent during much of the ordeal. Nor was it any fault of James that his father was incarcerated when his presence was needed most. It was about five years ago when I called upon the services of a governmental colleague to locate James Colquhoun, still my same age. He has a family of his own now as it happens. A son and twin daughters. And I wonder about that. I wonder about that rather intently."

Then, without anticipating a response, M directed his attention to the plate in front of him and began eating the food that had since cooled off. And as I stared across the table at the man who may very soon become the leader of this country, wondering what possible reason he might have had for telling me the story he just did, I couldn't help but imagine how closely he must have resembled his own father in this exact moment.

# XXX

## PRURIENCE

"Do you consider yourself a sexual person, Lawrence?"

"Nah–nah–nah not really, no."

"Coward."

A slight uneasiness lays its soft and sweatered arms over my collarbone. My response to the parliamentarian's prodding was pure and I was content to leave it at that, unexcavated and light, disintegrating toward the doldrums I was once forced to read about. No such peace granted for me today as Montblanc provides an addendum to his feathery insult.

"What can you truly know of yourself when you deny your own carnality?"

"I think mmm-my denying, my denying pr-pr-pr-probably says a lot."

"You are acutely self-aware, my friend, but a coward nonetheless. I won't subject you to further inquiries regarding your own sins of flesh, but with your permission I would like to share with you some of the more striking examples of the fascinating sexual appetites of my political colleagues, for there is a lesson to be learnt that may well enhance your understanding of this confection I myself must navigate."

Guilt, guilt, guilt, and then shame, as I was in my mind so eager to assure MM that this was, at this very moment in time, exactly what I wanted to hear. 'Yes, please tell me all you can of the particularly perverse presentations of politically perpetrated prurient power that occur in the world of the elite.' I'm fine-tuned, feeding on alien frequencies that describe a world I could never inhabit. Press my face up to the glass and allow me to gawk wide-eyed at the rituals and habits of the uninhibited. Don't reach over the fence. Don't throw things into the cage. Don't make direct eye contact. Follow these rules and a good, family-friendly time is guaranteed to all. Yes Mr. Mole, pray tell me all you can. But wait—modesty, my oldest friend, perhaps I should invite you into this party, that you might keep my frothing mouth wiped and clean.

"If-if-if-if if you think this is imp-imp-important . . ."

"Ah, young voyeur, I knew there resided a dancer within you yet. Very well, but no true names, lest I become the monster I am so often made out to be. And Lawrence?"

"Yes?"

"No interruptions."

And with that, Big M began regaling me with tales of the licentious tastes of his esteemed parliamentary peers. Mozart's *Eine kleine Nachtmusik*, however on the nose, still strikes me as the most appropriate for those playing conductor at home.

★★★

### *"John", Age: 54. Political Party: Conservatives*

A married and by all means a wealthy member of parliament, John willfully put his entire personal and professional careers in jeopardy when he entered into a virtual arrangement with a sexually precocious nineteen-year-old on the other side of the country. Relatively innocent in its inception, John would pay this young entrepreneur via credit card for her services, at the time nothing more than private camera shows. For a set price, our young temptress would provide an hour of her time on the camera, dancing, stripping, talking dirty, masturbating, whatever John's particular nighttime fancy happened to be. Initially it was her youth, her attractiveness, and her wise-beyond-her-years approach to seduction that appealed to John, but soon an indecent inciting incident occurred that excited him in a way welcomingly unfamiliar. She, with his credit card number on file, decided to buy herself a gift—a lamb skin shoulder bag with an impressive price tag attached. When John confronted her about this unagreed charge, she assured him that not only did she deserve this gift, but he would certainly be buying her many more. After all, she knew who he was, and it would be quite the controversy should his wife or his thousands of constituents find out about their salacious engagements. And with that threat she awoke something in John that had been lying dormant for some time. You see, his immediate reaction was not to change his credit card number, or confess to his wife, or involve law enforcement, rather, he reacted instead by masturbating in a manner so furious and so vigorous that the vitality and untenable urges of his youth returned to him in full insatiable force. From that moment on he obliged to every demand she made, whether it be buying her gifts, paying her rent, her university tuition—she had planned on attending law school after finishing her under-graduate degree, bless her heart—while also providing her with more personal information as she demanded it. His home address, his office location, the name and contact details of his secretary, the school his children attended, and of course, he allowed her to record all their lovingly consensual virtual meetings so in the event that she ever needed to incriminate or expose him it would be easy for her to do. John felt euphoric that a nineteen-year-old girl could, whenever she felt like doing so, destroy everything that he had worked to build, a euphoria that provided him access to orgasms with an intensity that he in his comfortable age had forgotten were possible, while she—only two years older than his own daughter—held the legitimacy of his life in one of her tiny hands, simultaneously using the other to orchestrate the crescen-do of his sexual reawakening.

### *"Jack", Age: 31, Political Party: Liberals*

One of our younger members in the House of Commons, Jack had previously dabbled in the craft of emotional abuse with past partners, though not to particularly noteworthy levels of severity. Though far from perfect—not physically violent, but with something of a temper—Jack and his fiancé had, for the most part, skirted the potential pitfalls of modern romance, opt-ing to keep their increasingly aggressive boudoir experimentation mutually consensual. It was a muggy June afternoon when Jack's fiancé received the phone call she had anticipated but hoped would never come. 'Grandma didn't make it.' She had wished to be there in person for this cross-country ordeal to say her last goodbye, but the haste with which it all happened complicated her best intentions and travel plans. Powerless and distraught, her tears introduced themselves without delay upon ending the short phone call as she looked to her betrothed for the unfiltered support he was expected to deliver during such times. But, by the absence of divinity, undelivered it was to remain.

Her tears—which he could rightly count on one hand the number of times he had seen previous, for she was a notoriously strong woman, seemingly impervious to expectation—had fostered in him a medley of mixed emotion beginning with a soft overture of curiosity before shifting seamlessly into the main movement of contempt. She must be truly hurting inside. 'How pitiful', thought he. He wondered what he might say to hurt her even more, to further widen the schism in her once invulnerable floodgates. A careful balance needed to be maintained, for any words that were conspicuously direct would surely illicit anger, and not the despair that he inexplicably craved.

'Grandma was probably wondering why you weren't there. That was probably her last thought.'

As Jack commenced down this line, the tears of his lovely fiancé flowed freer still. Not a particularly elegant man in the way of articulating his feelings, I doubt he could explain to you or I why her tears and his continued torment of her satisfied him so. Nevertheless, he continued.

'You know people shit themselves when they die. Do you think she was wearing a diaper at the time? What a humiliating way to go.'

And there was his once strong fiancé, collapsed in a leaking pile on the floor, hugging her knees as she wrestled simultaneously with her bereavement and with her bewilderment at the actions of the man whose name she was soon to take.

'It's okay, babe, your family doesn't really like you that much anyway right? I'm sure nobody missed you. The senile old bitch probably wouldn't have even recognized you.'

Jack's erection was now visibly protruding from his shorts on this muggy June afternoon as he set about pleasuring himself with his unwavering gaze fixated on the broken object before him. Several hours later he would successfully argue that his actions were the result of confusion and shock. Apologies, please understand. She didn't, but just a trip, not a fall.

Two months later I sat in the second row of their wedding ceremony, during which the beautiful bride let not free a single tear.

★★★

A brief silence meets us as, thoroughly engrossed, I use my eyes to encourage the storyteller to continue.

"Tell me, Lawrence, have you noticed a particular theme shared between these two examples?"

"I think, I think so."

I hadn't.

"Well, I'd rather not cautiously flirt with the idea so I'll be direct. The theme is power. It permeates everything"

I can see now that Monty is keen on making a point, venerably sharpened to a lethal tip as he was so often wont to do. But in this instance I'd rather he didn't. Truth is, my embarrassing thirst for sexual gossip had yet to be quenched. 'Tell me more, Max, I know we've only just covered the tip of this lascivious iceberg, and I'm so enjoying this glimpse into your strangely engrossing world.' Still, best to indulge him, I suppose.

"W–w–what do you mmmmmm–muh–mean by that?"

"I myself lost my virginity at the age of thirteen to my eighth-grade science teacher. Understand? She taught me of the physical world during class time before proceeding to do the same in a more extracurricular manner. My intellectual virginity, on the other hand, was to remain in tact for a number of years yet. Power. It permeates everything."

A moment passes before the ribald raconteur demonstrates his own powers of perception.

"Your eyes explicate your intentions, Lawrence. You're inclined to hear more, aren't you?"

I was. I point a half-smile in his direction and we share an unvoiced look of secret culpability.

"Very well. But I will caution you against absorbing my words as mere entertainment. Far be it from me to assume responsibility for your moral education, but do remember that a theme is under examination here. And what theme am I referring to?"

"Puh-puh-power."

"It permeates everything. *Alors*, let us carry on."

★★★

*"Jim", Age: 40, Political Party: Conservatives*

Unlike you or I, Jim's thirst was never quenched by the water of small-town wells. He is a true metropolitan, born and raised amid the social squalor and blasé desensitization that only ferments in the space between skyscrapers. As such, Jim was not accustomed to the company of any animals beyond cats, dogs, rats, and pigeons. He'd never looked his dinner in the eyes and he'd never needed to. A bully on the playgrounds of his youth, he had transitioned—quite successfully—his aggression into the business world, securing for himself a cozy net worth that helped secure his seat in parliament. Jim's sexual disposition was relatively tame, and while he occasionally called upon the services of escorts, his sessions with them were generally of a vanilla nature. His darker perversions first saw light during a campaign stop at a farm on the outskirts of his jurisdiction.

It was a goat that teased the evil actions that would soon become habitual. A curious goat that continued to harmlessly run its head against Jim's blue-jeaned leg. A winsome scene that made for a successful photo opportunity. Though he smiled through the ordeal while under the camera's gaze, once no eyes remained, his annoyance progressed to action. Jim delivered a light kick to the goat's side in an attempt to shoo him away, but the goat continued his cranial affront against his leg. More intrigued than annoyed now, Jim kicked the goat again, a little harder each successive time. This cycle continued for some time until Jim finally approached the farmer and inquired into the cost of a young goat. $300 a head. Was that it? And I can do anything I want to them once they're mine? Shortly thereafter Jim had worked out an arrangement with the farmer. When time permitted he would visit the farm and pay $600 cash for one young kid and for the farmer's compliance.

And what would Jim do with these goats he would purchase? He had sampled a few arrangements to varying degrees of success, but the one he found most effective was to simply wrap his legs around the goat, ensuring that it couldn't escape, and repeatedly slap it in the face and occasionally the testicles. The more the goat struggled, the harder he would hit, finding ecstasy in the pained bleats. When he tired of this, he would lift the goat above his head and throw it down to the ground with as much force as he could manage, usually stunning the creature in the process. Occasionally they would attempt to run away at this point—Jim liked it when they did this and they never made it far. At this point he would usually grab the goat by its hind legs, swinging it around and eventually smashing it on the ground once again. A few more kicks, and the finale—a stomp to the head—and Jim's session, now a monthly affair, would come to an end. I can't say for certain whether the pleasure he found in this activity was immediately sexual, though it nevertheless helped satisfy those inescapably familiar desires.

★★★

I feel my curiosity transition into disgust as the garrulous gossiper finishes his story. I want to stop this now. I want to go back to work. I don't want to do this anymore. I'm a kid who's eaten too much candy. I'm naked eyes staring at the sun. I am Lazarus, reanimated with a hole where my headache should go. My uneasiness is apparently not a well-kept secret.

"Forgive me, Larry, but do recall a fundamental lesson of Ecclesiastes—with much wisdom comes much sorrow. Power is not something we may inconsequentially accumulate; it is a spire that demands additional nails be driven into our feet with every significant elevation. And what of I, now within grasp of the most powerful political position one can openly attain in this country? Have I not engaged in acts of obscenity more potent or troubling than any of those I have described to you today? Some say that power resembles a muscle in need of consistent exercise. I myself do not fully subscribe to this line of thought, though I do see the merits in this metaphor. Regardless, if there is one lesson that I may leave with you on the subject of power, it would be what?"

"It puh–puh–puh, it puh–permeates everything."

"And I suspect that the libido is as good a place to start as any other. Remember, my dear side-lined dancer, there are doers and there are watchers, but only one of these camps may retain any confidence in the constitution of their soul."

## 31

# PUERILITY

SERENDIPITOUS SECONDS THESE. Can't recall the formula I used to make it this far, but I'll be damned if I watch this payload sink to the bottom of the Pacific. I'll dive in myself. 1991 Pontiac Sunbird. Make friends, if you will, with the burn marks on the bedroom carpet. Catch a few drops of cerebral sodium and feel the burn on your red right arm. Done fucking with the concoction yet? Play me a sad one, Joe, guide me toward the aural tranquility that I am damn-well entitled to. Too close to the ovens, the cloth slugs crawling on my shoulder, sticking with the heat. They don't make them like the used to. Stay the fuck away from my windshield. I called the number on the back just after midnight, no breathing on the other side. Doesn't matter so long as we can keep the good graces vibrating. In preparation for my long escalator ride to heaven I've been practicing the lost art of standing motionless. My mind wanders and my paltry little legs shortly follow. Now you've done it. Rest, reset, resist, rejoice, resplendence. Standing in line to pick up a package. The useless fuck working the desk moves as if any sign of efficiency is a crime against humanity. Take it home, jet black coffee. I don't have to be here.

Fuck off, I don't have to be here. Fuck Maxime Montblanc and fuck his memoirs. I want to write the Great Canadian pop-up book instead. You with me?

# 32

## PAEDOTROPHY

SEE MONTBLANC THE iconoclast draped snug in the skins of yesterday's men, the men we were meant to believe as righteous. There is not enough in his words alone to define him. His list of deeds runs long and reads like an epic of human potential. I observe and I learn what I can but even with my insider advantage I am forced to extrapolate. My portrait of the man is to be reserved and subdued but I wonder on the stories that could be told were my hands not stayed by the grey palate and weak constitution of the masses. For example, I had read that at some point in his life the good *Monsieur* was a volunteer Scouts leader. Knowing what I do about the man I found this difficult to believe, yet he confirmed this when I asked, though he shared no more on the subject claiming it had no relevance to the book. He's probably right, though I still find myself dreaming up visions of what that must have looked like. I think I'm familiar enough with his voice now to conjure up an accurate enough depiction.

The way I see it, M is standing in a small forest clearing as his preadolescent Scouts are knelt facing him in a semi-circular formation. His lecture is hypnotic and he speaks to the children as if they were adults, showing them respect enough to not deemphasize his words or the messages contained within. The children listen in stern discipline, eager to impress their towering leader as he orates and pontificates on the lessons of the day:

*On Perseverance, Praising Softly, Dispossessed Wallows*
Breathe deep the oxygen of these woods my young cubs and know that in the summer of 1970 when I shared your current age

there was but ash to surround you. The quantity and severity of the forest fires that year remains unmatched. I remember walking through the naked and skeletal trees, my feet disappearing in their remains. Look again and see what you will. The boundless fertility beneath the erect pines mayhap? How can this exist when I can still recall the graveyard that occupied the same locale? I remember the thickness of the smoke filling my lungs and reddening my eyes and the orange horizon that lit the night sky. The evacuation was swift, though in their panic and haste none of the retreating townsfolk thought to check on the wheelchair-bound Madame Wagner. She lived alone, confined to her stark home. Her remains were found several days later rested on top her bed. And now in the place where here home used to be? A multi-story townhouse complex.

Yes, the fires that summer roared with an ardent ferocity that you should all hope to feel within yourselves one day. But if you could ask the trees here if they can feel their predecessors sap boiling with them, what would they say? And here I ask you more importantly still, does it warrant consideration either way? Who amongst you can in honesty say that they would stand as tall after having walked with the heat of Hell's fire blazing at your back?

### On Power, the Obscured Hand that Steers

Power needn't be seismic in its exercise or display save for those who would in ignorance or complacency shut their eyes to it. Look around and see one another. Each and all of you know well your approximate place in the manner of things. What if I told you that there are only provisions enough to feed one of you tonight? What if I told you that I wanted you all to take to the pit with naught but your fists and your wits and that only the last one of you standing would be fed tonight? Now see it plain as I do and dwell on these invisible calculations of power. You know which of your peers you could knock down. You know which of your peers could best you. These dispositions existed before I called your thoughts to them and they will exist indefinitely after. Power is understood tacitly and this is when it is most conducive to order. Only when doubts in these relationships arise can this order be challenged.

But the implications of *true* power will always appear as inevitabilities. True, I could force you all to fight for food tonight—and you would do it, even though provisions are not limited and even though should you all band together you could easily restrain me and take whatever you wanted. But not one among you even considered this as a possibility. That, my young cubs, is the horror of true power.

### *On Continence, the Binding of Ankles, Cracks in the Pavement*

Listen close to any room and the voice of the cleverest person therein will remain unknown to you. For what can they say that is but evasive to the efforts of dullened tools? Loudness in volume will not replace the respect you will all develop. It will come gradual and impervious to measurement, but it will come, for yours are the pedigrees of elasticity and malleability. And should you find yourselves perched above common earshot you will by then know better than to forfeit your days looking beneath you for signs of compatible life. Were I on record I might say that you could binarize your existence into things that need to be done and things you are currently doing and suggest that these paths should most often be intertwined. But no, my cubs, for the absence of words is preferable to those which are wasted.

### *On Empathy, Becoming Halos, Moral Cartography*

Listen well to this final lesson for it supersedes all others in importance and in urgency. Know that only recently have I found this to be true, and rejoice that you might enjoy the fruits of my discovery at a such an enviable and advantageous age. And the lesson is this . . . Find a ghostwriter, find someone to tell your story! I got a guy and he's literally the best. He's so talented and awesome and what's more, he's my friend and I just respect him so darn much. Seriously, kids, I may be rich and successful and wear nice clothes and talk fancy, but I'm still not as badass as this dude is. I'm so blessed that he came into my life and I wish you all could find someone like him to make your worlds awesome too!

Okay, so I might have lost his voice toward the end there, but other than that I think I did a pretty good job capturing Montblanc's diction. It's almost noon and I haven't done a damn thing today.

# 33

## PROCIDENCE

I LACKED THE tact to think to call him 'doctor.' I was counting the numbers well before they were organized sequentially. I think that the anesthetic maybe isn't working as intended sir. She's getting out of bed again. Montblanc says to omit that part. I am not a journalist. I have no obligation to the truth. I say 'okay' as if I have any agency at all. There are no brands on my bones. Tomorrow's archaeologists have already forgotten about me. What would the Ouija say if she could see us now? We were never particularly graceful. Rest, rest, Lucifer lacked the foresight for us. Sundered up the sins of our past, makeshift sutures too lax to last. I happen to already know how this chicanery ends—with me wandering the southern states of America for a place to call home. With the doctor's permission, I would like to remove her from these squalid conditions. Some might say she deserves better and I count myself among their ranks. On the twentieth of July, in the year of our Lord 2012, Montblanc, while still maintaining sufficient influence from behind the lunar curtains, relinquished official operational control of his company to a trusted associate he had worked with for nearly two decades. On whatever the hell day it is today, I managed to hold my breath for exactly one minute while M's microwave warmed my burrito with its radiating hug.

I need to get out of this damn house. It's raining for the first time since I've arrived.

## 34

## PECCADILLOES

MONTBLANC SAT UPRIGHT at a circular table in the corner of a London hotel lounge with his back to the wall. From this vantage he could slightly redirect his eyes upward from the organized mess of papers in front of him to see all comers and goers and this he did. He had been surveying his presentation notes for the duration of near three glasses of blood-red wine and was content in his mind with his current level of preparedness. His oratory eloquence was often deemed as a gift of inheritance, and perhaps it was, but he nevertheless supplemented this with sufficient review and preparation—he only did so from the safety of inconspicuous corner tables where he might remain incognito, another foreign transient of no importance. The playlist of the evening— a disimpassioned mix of piano-driven jazz tracks curated and organized by the artificial hands of some algorithm—played now at a volume just gracious enough to allow the essences of surrounding conversations to seep through the air to curious ears. Montblanc took visual roll call of the room as he had long since trained himself to do.

Straight down his field of vision were the two Poles. They had been there since before Montblanc arrived and were drinking at a heroic pace which served no explicit purpose beyond allowing them to drink more still. The Poles were incapable of remaining sat for any extended amount of time and they alternated uneasily and loudly between sitting, standing, and obambulating closely within the orbit of their table. Speaking Polish, they were engaged in a fervent discussion, the volume of which superseded all others in the room. To those not privy the two red-faced men seemed locked in cyclical

verbal confrontation that might at any moment erupt into
blows.

The American had announced his nationality first through
his attire—jeans and a black tee shirt with the logo of some company not worth knowing adorned to its front—and second
through his inexperience with the environment's folkways. He
sat at the bar drinking from a glass the only beer he recognized
on the taps. He drank clumsily and gauchely as if the glass were
a baby's bottle filled with formula. When he paid for his drinks
he fumbled through a handful of British notes, the colours and
their respective denominations unfamiliar to him. He was far
from home.

Two tables to Montblanc's left sat a man and a woman also
enjoying the relative privacy afforded by the room's corner. The
woman in a black dress and speaking with a British accent, the
man in a maroon sweater with an accent Montblanc recognized
as Australian. The woman had excused herself from the table several times and when she did the man would look down through
his glasses and fixate on his cellphone until she would return several minutes later.

Tending bar tonight was a short and young brown-skinned
man with a hairstyle Montblanc had never seen before. The night
was slow and the barman walked from one end of the long wood
to the other cleaning arbitrarily and engaging in other menial
tasks between sips of carbonated water. The Poles conversed
loudly. The American searched for a TV screen. The Australian
waited patiently. Montblanc danced a slow waltz routine in his
head.

At this moment another man enters the lounge. He scans the
mostly empty room until he locks eyes with Montblanc. The
man is not wearing the standard employee garb of the hotel, but
seems to have a familiarity with the establishment. He makes his
way to Montblanc's table, cautiously maneuvering around the
Poles who were standing and swaying and flailing with near-
empty glasses in hand.

"Everything to your liking so far, Mr. Montblanc?"

"Quite nice indeed, thank you."

The Poles, still partnered in stentorian dialogue, had approached the bar to replenish their refreshments. The larger of the two men twice smacked the palm of his hand down on the wood in front of him and gestured to his glass that was empty save for some partially melted ice cubes.

"I've arranged for your transportation to the venue tomorrow morning. A driver will meet you in the lobby at eight."

"And until then?"

"If you would prefer company tonight, that can quickly be arranged."

The barman, professionally masking any disapproval he may have felt with the lumbering men on the other side of his wood, produces two fresh glasses of vodka topped with water and tells them the price. The same price as before. And the time before that. As the Pole on the left pays, the one on the right gracelessly extends his arm across the bar for a napkin, spilling the drink that had just been placed in front of him. The glass falls over the edge of the bar, emptying its contents on the shirt and pants of the American before falling to the carpeted floor.

"No, I should like to be alone tonight, though I do have something of a shopping list."

"Of course, anything you need."

The American raises both arms above his head as small cubes of ice slip off his jeans and onto the floor. The barman instinctively reaches for a clean cloth and hands it to the American who was still undecided as to how he might react. He stands up and brushes the remaining ice off his thighs. The innocent Pole begins to laugh a donkey laugh as his partner invades the American's proximity.

"Will you be using all of this?"

"That's irrelevant. Can you get it or not?"

The Pole, inches now from the American, bends down to retrieve the unbroken glass from the carpet. He places it on the bar and, making eye contact with the barman, points to it several times. As the barman takes the glass the Pole uses his thumb to point at the American while simultaneously reaching into his back pocket. The Australian watches silently from the corner.

"Of course, Mr. Montblanc. Is there anything else at all I can do for you?"

"In fact there is. See those two?"

The barman hastily mixes two new drinks that the Pole pays for. He raises his glass to the American who mirrors the gesture.

"Those two?"

"Mhmm."

Through their language barrier, the Pole and the American share a drink.

"You're sure?"

"Just take care of it."

The Poles return to their table and resume their thunderous conversation. The American is still slightly damp and still far from home.

"Of course, my apologies, Mr. Montblanc, it will be done, and please do feel free to reach out if you need anything else at all tonight."

"Good night then."

The man stands up and leaves. Montblanc does not watch him go. He takes the glass of wine to his lips and closes his eyes for only a moment. Revelry underscores the images on the back of his eyelids and all is exempt and untaxed. The aura generated from the room sat weightless, floating on top clear water of some rarefied purity. Montblanc did not believe in auras. A new darkness fell as he placed his hands over his shut eyes and rubbed them up and down. The purple silhouettes of butterflies and flown-over swamps blinking and disappearing and it may have lasted for all time under any opposing definitions of consciousness. There were no frontiersmen of note that sat in the lounge of this airport hotel. They would not ride out at first light to the sound of horseshoes on the tarmac. They would not trespass the holy lands of the natives nor lay with their women. Montblanc removed his hands from his face and opened his eyes. The Australian was speaking to the British girl who was feigning interest enough. The American was still far from home.

And here did Montblanc remain for a length of time no one seemed to be counting until two new men arrived. They entered the lounge and though they immediately recognized Montblanc sitting wistfully in the corner, they did not outwardly acknowledge his presence. Instead they proceeded directly to the Poles and without a single wasted action each took grip of a Pole, locking their necks with their arms and turning an even darker shade their already reddened faces. The Poles dropped their drinks while kicking and throwing unfocused punches behind their heads. They grunted and wheezed as they were dragged out of the lounge. The patrons watched on, mouths agape, eyes unblinking. The barman knew better than to ask questions. The British woman had her hand over her mouth and the Australian sat in silence. The American was still far from home. They all watched on as the Poles were carried out of the building and into the cool night.

They all watched on save for Montblanc, who did not once avert his eyes from the notes in front of him. He finished his glass of wine and calmly retired to his room on the sixth floor.

# 35

## PACIFICATION

I'M STILL TRYING to save you, Edie. I know there's still a heaven for us. While I have never met you in this life I have often envisioned how our first night might have transpired. You're sitting in the corner of a room that I have no business being in. I'm a country-boy with no experience in that world, but maybe that would have been novelty enough to get me through the door. Either way, you're sitting there in the corner with one leg flat on the floor and the other bent up with your arm resting on it. In one hand burns a cigarette, in the other a clear glass half-filled with vodka. You've kept a smile on your face that draws me in on every stolen glance. You laugh and I can't help but smile when I see your dimples and your eyes and your teeth. You laugh and the whites of your eyes disappear under your dark and heavy makeup. I don't care for the smell of second-hand smoke, yet I find your continuous drags endearing. I've heard that you were a bit of a lush, but you seem to be composing yourself with the elegance of someone who is used to having all eyes in the room focused on them. And in that moment, I am awe. I am the character in a story that my heart could never bear to read. And I see ours with crystalline precision and inevitable conclusion.

But I can get you to eat, Edie. I know I can. I want you to feel as strong and beautiful as you were made to. No, I'll rub my hands across your flat chest and your ribcage and the notches of your spine and I will promise to always touch whatever you offer. Please eat, Edie, you will still be light enough to fly. You won't need to search for your wings anymore. I know they've hurt you before, Edie. I know why you wear your heart short, your hair shorter, and your wits so close. I know the size and weight of the burden you carry on your narrow shoulders, your 103-pound frame refusing to buckle, but you don't have to drink it away tonight, Edie. Tonight, we are reborn into summer skies. Every time you say the beauty mark on your cheek is ugly I will kiss it twice. I've known the imitators Edie and not one of them are fit to model your clothes.

Edie, I know there are scars on your body. I know where they cut into your uterus and I don't condemn you. I know that they took you to the hospital Edie, but I will wait for you every time, you will always have a ride home. I know the pills feel good Edie, but so do many other things, I know I can show you.

I know that you died during the morning of November 15, 1971 at the age of twenty-eight. I know it's too late to save you, Edie, but still I'm trying. I'm still searching for my wings so that I may meet you yet. Because I know you can fly, Edie, and I know there's still something worth smiling about.

I know there's still a heaven for us where we can hold on and never let go.

# 36

## PETRICHOR

*Save me, O God! For the waters are come in unto my soul.*
*I sink in deep mire, where there is no standing:*
*I am come into deep waters, where the floods overflow me.*

*Psalms 69: 1-2*

THIS RAIN IS not letting up. Three days later and the deluge continues. For three days now we have felt the force of this rain as it assaults my rooftop and cuts through spider webs. And I ask you, Lawrence, are we content with this fate revealed before us? Could you find the bravery within you to face the unbridled arsenal of the atmosphere? And it would rain then, as it is raining now. Whatever choices are to us today free were surely ungraspable then.

I was ten years old, a subject of the diocese of Bishop Fergus O'Grady, spanning across the entirety of the largely uninhabited lands of Northern British Columbia. Though they would never say what it was that made them leave, my parents would often tell me stories of their previous life in Quebec, of the connectedness of the Catholic community there, and of the outside world that conspired against them. Enter the empire of Fergus O'Grady—the Bulldozer Bishop—so named because of the amount of land he would convert into suitable grounds for Catholic schools. As I understand he would often operate the land-shaping machinery personally. A blessing to my parents that I might retain a properly pious education under the tutelage of Bishop O'Grady's Frontier Apostolate.

And it would rain then, out on the schoolyard, as it is raining now.

*Stand out in the rain Maxime. Feel God's gift. Do not struggle against it.* Palms upturned toward the sky, everyone's heart so filled with God's love. Please—enough—there's a four-walled promise of safety escaping in the distance. I can't hold my arms up any higher than this. They would never believe that. Have you any powers in you to make these rains stop, Lawrence? You haven't. And nor did I. I felt heavy under the downpour as if I were sinking into the wet ground. What I wanted then was the safety of an enclosed space. Away from the rain, away from their eyes. My developing body defenseless under the weight of my wet clothes, my arms ordered to remain raised toward Heaven. And their eyes. And they are getting closer still. I pray that no one can tell the difference between the rain and the tears. Our drenched uniforms clinging to our bodies, forms made bare. Even then I knew how well-endowed I was. And so too did they.

My parents are dead now. Underground. Made soft by the rain. A congealed mush like old leaves in a gutter. Water has no memory and I refuse to believe that they are speaking to me through this rhythmic downpour. But switches exist on the control panel of memory, and they are depressed now by the curious force of these oversized drops. And they live again. And their piety lives again. And God speaks again, His voice muffled, scattered amid the cloudburst.

And their veins would still be devoid of the milk of human kindness.

The blackness inside my father, they say it pulled his strings, it made him do things that he wouldn't have done. By the time His end had come, I had long since made a point of not being around him. I knew that without hesitation, He would have transferred His demon invader unto me. And no amount of God's rain would be able to wash that away. Oh, but there is a hunger within me, Lawrence. To push aside the walls, to break the glass of the windows, to ram the door down. They are dead and not coming back, and not a moment too soon. Would they be pleased to know that I have a $900 umbrella that I now use to shield my head from the falling rain. Do you want it? I no longer need it. I want to feel the water on my head. I want to feel it running down my face. I fear I cannot stay in here much longer. Oceans apart from what was expected of me. But what man lets the chaos of weather dictate his course? A weak man. A cretinous and unrefined boor and his miserable cow of a wife, both convinced that no handrails were needed on the path God had provided. The same path set before me, corralling me toward the same mundane and frivolous fate.

Eventually this rain will end and bring about a pleasant scent. The entrails of snails assailing the bottom of my shoes. The ignominious end of their path. Befitting of those who only come out during the rain. See what they get for it. Still, God continues to love all His creatures. You, me, Bishop O'Grady, the snails, the cur whose seed arrived me, the masquerading misanthrope who for nine months carried it. But you, Larry, my privy praiser, you of course know how easily the love of God may be lost in translation. The lyrics of your ode need only relay what can otherwise be found on government documents. Add to this your established literary flair but not one thought more.

Maintain the image. For what else is democracy but the pinnacle of idolatry?

# 37

## PRIVATION

AND LO, THERE I was, sent to the mountains for my crimes against what the tallest man in the room called the natural way. As I crossed the wooden bridge into the lands of white-capped spires, the black-clad men who were to be my compeers of iniquity remained in silence. Silence, as I would soon come to know, was the *lingua franca* of my new family. And silence did claim its superiority. The timbre of my voice a distant ripple behind the rudder of silence. The thoughts I once used to confirm my being, the deluded compulsions of my heart, all blanketed now by the icy quilt of silence and sleet. With naught to hear now but the dirge of the mountain's black winds I may freely focus on the compunction I was meant to have.

And silence will remain.

Each morning frost forms on our joints and mobility is stifled. The more experienced men here move at a pace that would make reintroduction into the former world an impossibility. Their feet never leave the ground as they shuffle their way through the fresh-fallen snow. These were men who once could run. Men who once could chase. And they did. Now their muscles have diminished, their range of movement curtailed by the gelid braces on their legs. I too have felt the slow disintegration of my body's potency with each passing moon. Very soon the agility that I once relied upon to carry out the odious ambitions of my broken mind will be gone from me and I will become prone prey for the bone-breaking beasts that inhabit these rimy peaks.

And stillness will remain.

On these peaks, we suffer the constant irony of being the tallest men on Earth. We who have strayed in perverse ways from what is right were now closer to the sun than anyone else. And soon did we discover that the sun's bounty is rationed per the inescapable tenets of justice, for it was not warmth it provided, but judgement. The blank canvases of snow refracted the sun's light into our eyes whenever they were open, and soon we were faced with a choice. We could eventually blind ourselves from continual ultraviolet exposure, or we could keep our eyes closed as our minds ought to have been. I chose to keep my eyelids shut, and shortly thereafter, I had forgotten how to open them altogether. It was vision that initially allowed us to covet, and so too must vision be sacrificed in the name of righteousness.

And sightlessness will remain.

The vociferous thoughts that brought us here begin to vacate our minds. Released from the burdens of sight and sound we are blessed now with the opportunity to dwell undisturbed on the recklessness of our past choices. And soon did such thoughts consume us. The thinness of the air prevents a proper intake of oxygen, still, the lungs struggle to regulate, unaware and blameless of the reasons that brought them to such heights. There is no longer a distinction between night and day. We expend only the energy required to keep our minds stable enough for thoughts of repentance. After only my first month on the world's peak, I have lost the need for sleep. I use what hours would have been wasted in rest to continue my passage inward. I am all that is sinister in this life, and I will discover why.

And sleeplessness will remain.

So, frozen we are to stay, far above the heartbeat of humanity, far removed from the desecration we have wrought. No monuments to our existence to be found on these frigid crowns, we live now only to consider our own disgrace. Though torturous thoughts of subversion will at times slip through. About my black-cloaked cohabitants, were they not once counted among those below? Before the silence, the stillness, the sightlessness, the sleeplessness, did we not have the freedom to fail and to err? But these are dangerous thoughts to be ignored. I shift my focus instead to where it is meant to be. To the transgression that lead to my banishment. To the action that caused the tallest man to sentence me to the snowy apex where I will forever remain.

## 38

## PUTSCHIST

ON LOSS AND on where did it all go? Tonight I convinced myself that I had lost all of M's book. All the files, all the notes, all the drafts, graphs, and charts. Everything gone, and now I can't sleep. There's no way to replicate any of that work. It's gone. I'm back to square one. Eyes unclosing, I first considered this as an opportunity to instead tell the story of Montblanc's latest kill.

★★★

FADE IN
INT. DIMLY LIT BASEMENT—NIGHT
The basement floor is covered in a thin layer of sawdust. Three men; M, D, and R, stand in a semi-circle, their backs facing the camera, obstructing our view of their captive. R, 45, a thin, clean-shaven man still wearing his well-fitting pea coat breaks the unsettling silence.

                    R
        You're sure this is the guy?


                    D
            Positive.


                    R
    And you're sure nobody is gonna miss him?

                         D
           Can't ever be sure of that.


                         R
           You know what I mean.


                         D
           Then yeah, I'm sure.


                         R
           Well boss, he's your game,
       how do you want to go about it?


                         M
          Brothers, surely his mouth
             must first be filled.


D and R mumble in agreement and step aside,
revealing their captive, LAWRENCE SIERRA MANN,
30. Stripped naked and visibly emaciated,
LAWRENCE desperately looks around the room for
something that might help save him - but between
you and me, luck won't be on his side for the
remainder of this exchange.


                         M
           Take off your sock R,
        just the left one should do.


R does as instructed. He had worn white socks that
day, normally not the decision of one concerned
with fashion, but the blisters on his feet had
recently opened, and he quite enjoyed altering
this pure shade with the crimson colours of his
puss and blood. It had been near seven weeks since
R had deflowered a virgin and his inner tensions
were starting to manifest in curious ways.

M
That's it. Now into his mouth. All of it.

R attempts to stuff his soiled sock into the
mouth of the restrained LAWRENCE. It doesn't
quite fit like it should.

M
Come now, all of it.

Using two fingers, R jams the cultured cotton
down the sensitive throat of LAWRENCE. His gut-
tural gagging elicits the attention of D, the
more sympathetic of the trio.

D
Breathe through your nose, friend.
No sense in hurting yourself here.

LAWRENCE adheres to this advice, like a good lad
would.

M
Brothers, this man is a terrorist.

R
That right? You a terrorist?

LAWRENCE responds with a muffled protest.

R
You piece of shit. You camel-fucking,
towel-headed, sand-nigger piece of shit.
I should have known.

LAWRENCE attempts to protest louder, but the
unpleasantness of his forced meal tickles his

gag-reflex just right—his throat widens, and
vomit begins seeping out the sides of the tight
seal. GOD still loves him, and D removes the
sock long enough for him to catch his breath and
empty his stomach, which at this point contained
little more than acid and bile.

                        D
    Breathe the air, friend, but say one word
        and even I won't be able to help you.

                        R
            He's breathed long enough,
            let's get it back in.

R picks the sock up from the floor, dripping now
with stomach juice and sawdust, and reinserts it
into the mouth of LAWRENCE. In doing so, he gets
some vomit on his fingers, which he calmly wipes
off on LAWRENCE'S bare chest.

                        R
    Do you know what we do to terrorists here?
    Hmm? Do you know why the floor is covered
                in sawdust?

LAWRENCE hadn't had time to ponder the nurturing
nature of evil nor the specific reasons for his
current situation, though curiously, he did make
an immediate mental note of the sawdust on the
floor the second he was dragged into the room.
Might this have been a clue as to where he was?
Not as such. The dust wasn't natural, though
perhaps the reasoning behind it was. Inspired by
the callousness of his captors, LAWRENCE met the
moment with a dignified stoicism - the moment he
realized what indeed the sawdust was for. It's

good for catching the blood. Makes it easy to
clean.

                         M
      You were my embryo, but now you have gone
                 and buried the Bible.

                         D
              You've buried it, friend.

                         R
          A real fucking mess you made.
                Say, I have an idea.

                         M
                  Speak, brother.

                         D
                 Speak it, brother.

                         R
        I bet we can carve a cunt into him.
               I am an artist after all.

                         M
      How do they meet with treason out East, D?

                         D
              Enemies of the government?

                         R
           My cock can tell the difference.

LAWRENCE amuses himself. M speaks, then D
speaks, and then R. *Mort de rire.* LAWRENCE
thinks hard on that. He doesn't think about how
big the hole needed to be, or where it would go.

He holds on to his sense of humour and his
humanity with it. Surely a traitor or a terrorist would have abandoned that long ago, but not
LAWRENCE. Hope, it would seem, is not so easily
extinguished.

                    M
          And he smiles still.

                    D
        The cause is too important.

                    R
     Hey M, let me open him up a bit.

*Mort de rire* again. LAWRENCE smiles through the
sock. He smiles as the saliva dribbles down his
chin. He smiles as R approaches with the knife.

                    M
          You've buried the Bible.

                    D
              Buried it.

                    R
     I've only been fucking slants lately.
            This will be fun.

And the laughter comes. Reparations for stolen
land, for slanders against the KING. The blood
of saboteurs flowing through his veins, now
caught by the woodchips on the ground. Deeper in
it goes, and deeper from the belly comes the
laughter. Men were once quartered for the crime
of attempted regicide. Today we enjoy more civilized times. Knives are sharper. You can barely

feel them going in. It's when the sawing motion
starts when the niggling gives way to giggling.
And O, how LAWRENCE giggled and chortled! These
clowns didn't even bring enough sawdust! And as
LAWRENCE laughed notes he thought he had long
since lost, he saw parts of his flesh rebel
against his body. Hilarious irony! Though his
vision was blurring, LAWRENCE kept his eyes
open, open enough to see the towering M
approach.

                     M
              My weary embryo...
              Buried... Bible...
              And then nothing.
                FADE TO BLACK.


                    ★★★


But I didn't really lose M's book. It's still all there, on the
computer in the other room. It's been backed up to two different
external drives because that's the kind of person I am. Or was. It's
getting harder to tell. Maybe I should count some sheep.

One . . .
Two . . .
Three . . .
FADE TO BLACK.

# 39

## POINTILLISM

OFTENTIMES I LIKE to skim through the memoirs of famous political figures to draw inspiration, though I usually fail to make it
past their covers. Most of them are just so impossibly lame and
replicate the tired template of the subject photographed from the
shoulders up, staring at the camera and smiling enticingly. Maybe
I'm too close to the situation, but I can't envision Montblanc
posing like that. Or smiling enticingly for that matter. What kind
of cover is he going to use? How is he going to market his book
once I'm finished writing it? These decisions are beyond me. I'm
just a mule tasked with colouring and collaging the truth while
hitting the optimal word count. Too short and it will make his
achievements seem insubstantial, too long and it will turn off the
more casual of readers. There's a science to all things of this
nature. MaMo might just earn himself the Order of Merit one
day. You think maybe I could too?

I could dig that. Shit, I think I just disqualified myself.

Still, in that alternate reality a time will come for me to write
my own memoirs, and you can bet your last shiny quarter that
my cover won't suck ass like all those others. And you know
what else? That fucker will be as thick as a thigh and heavy
enough to remedy the largest of ganglion cysts. And it won't
have any polished fluff either. The whole thing will be an ency-
clopedic account of every fault, flaw, failing, foible, and fuck-up
that I can account.

Like the time I went to a house party when I was fifteen and,
after trying to impress the older kids outside by smoking three
cigarettes in a row, puked in the bathtub and blamed it on Chris
Evans who had conveniently passed out on the couch and was

unable to defend his honour. Or that time in ninth grade when I stealthily scoped out Kim Ribald as she typed in her email password, only to check her inbox later that day to find that she had told Aimee Woods that she thought I was gross and had bad hair. Or the fact that I, to this very day, can't sleep with my bedroom door closed because I get scared of what might be trapped in the room with me. Or the fact that I believed in Santa Claus far longer than any of my peers did because my dad once told me that I should believe whatever I wanted to believe. Or the fact that I constantly lie about having seen certain movies like *Schindler's List*. Or the fact that I call myself a writer but I still have no idea how to maintain a proper and cohesive narrative structure so I rely instead on postmodern experimentation in the hope that my subjects never realize that their emperor isn't wearing any clothes.

Fuck you, keep going.

I can't get out of bed most mornings. When I can, I stare at the hourglass behind the blank screen and wonder what will happen when the last grain of sand is finally funneled through. The increased ubiquity of online ordering is one of the best things that's ever happened in my lifetime. Some nights I can hear Montblanc tickling the keys of his piano with a feathery touch from the floor above me. I tried belonging to some online stuttering communities. They would share articles and treatments and stories of struggles and success. I found myself quickly despising them all. The querulousness of this queer modern year yearns to define us. Acceptance and defiance paint us with the same crusty brush.

You don't need a voice if you don't have anything worth saying.

## 40

## POLLICITATION

THERE'S NO KNOCK on my bedroom door before the unexpected M opens it and unhurriedly enters. There's always an unavoidable second or two of confusion whenever you're awoken in the middle of the night, particularly when you're in a foreign bed, and particularly when you're being awoken by a person you've never once before seen under this hour's light. Wait, what hour? I steal a glance toward the trusty electric clock, unchanged in design for decades, and its ever-stalwart LED lights of order. 3:17 am. Wow, what a time to be alive.

Max is anomalously underdressed, wearing only a purple robe. It looks to be quite nice—elegant even. Made of silk? Velour? Cotton? Not like I would even know. Forget it, the robe is purple, we can leave it at that. Let me gather my thoughts for a second here so I can process this. Damn, why is he here? Does he have some somnambulant habits he never told me about? Or maybe he's finally come to hold the pillow over my mouth and do me in proper? I know too much about him. He probably has a perfect hiding place for my body. Well the joke is on you, Monty, your book isn't even halfway finished yet. Good luck finding another ghostwriter who'll be willing to put up with these unscheduled late-night visits. Showing a touch of courtesy by leaving the light off, he turns his head toward me with unusual sheepishness and initiates our unrehearsed conversation.

"Apologies for waking you, Larry, but if I may confess, I find myself this morning in a curious state of arousal. Not sexually, as can so easily be remedied, but rather toward an untouchable and lost curiosity. Thinking in fantasies for a kiss, not mechanical and banal as when I used to greet my wife, but empathetic and tinged with the underused palette of excitement. Forgive my wandering mind, but in these occasionally listless early mornings it can be hard to parse out the influence of the dreamscapes recently left behind. If you are willing to indulge me for a moment I would like to continue on this path."

I must be getting better at interpreting the meaning of Montblanc's convoluted requests, as here I get the unfortunate sense that he wants to tell me about a dream that he just had. Is there anything more unfruitful for the receiving party then when a dream is relayed? Like some hack of an author he will describe to me a picture that I will likely interpret in a way incongruent with what he intended and I will be left to 'um and ah' with how to make sense of his symbols of uncontaminated subjectivity. 'Well, Max, I've heard that your teeth falling out in a dream can mean a great number of things. How was your relationship with your mother by the way?' Give me a break, does he really want to do this? I never figured him for one to prostitute his dreams for inspiration or conversation. A dishonest tactic utilized by the unskilled. No, wait. That's not fair. Lest I be crowned the grand King of Hypocrites I ought to remind myself that I've done the very same thing in this book. A dishonest tactic utilized by me. Dali gets a pass. Regardless, these are thoughts I keep to myself during my almost entirely disingenuous response.

"Yes, puh-puh-puh-please carry on."

"Thank you, Lawrence. My darling comrade. As I alluded, I have tonight been enveloped by the reverberant echoes of yesterday's footsteps. With eyes assuredly closed I saw her once again. Her, from an era of antiquity—before my name bared weight, before my thoughts given form. Her deep blue eyes to be sailed on, her onyx black hair to be individually counted in eagerness. A visage that nearly four decades ago could be found adjacent to mine. But more potently, her voice, delivering to me a vital message of palliation. I am today locked in position and increasing in speed, the burden of a man's ambition and choice. But then, a child physically, an uninitiated mentally, a thief amorously, and what made all the difference was the time with her.

"Tonight I saw her again.

"Her, who had slipped from common vision into the dusty recesses of memory. No time was wasted in renewing acquaintance as if we were both tacitly aware of the limited seconds afforded to us. We met in the same place where we used to all those years ago, under the conifers that comprised the area in-between civilized existences. Huddled with the trees in seclusion and burgeoning twilight, we reunited as the unseen keepers of a love half-understood. It was in this exact spot that thirty-nine years ago we made a promise to each other, and it was in the same spot that we met not one hour ago.

"She hadn't aged.

"Years of absence and now my mind is incapable of filling in the blanks. But her voice was heard with undiminished clarity, and her words delivered with familiar fervency. Though brief our exchange, to have seen that place again—those trees with the moonlight sifting through, the pinecones strewn across the ground where we sat, and her blue eyes focused on mine.

"Tonight I found her and attempted to make good on my word.

"She accepted my apologies with reassurance and warmth, and I felt a long-held burden break through my chest. In my new weightlessness I thanked her, and as the words came from my mouth I was pulled from our sanctuary back to the waking world like a newborn being pulled from the womb. I felt at once both empty and inspired, both longing and content, but was unable to close my eyes again. I needed to respect and pay due consideration to what had just happened, to this beautiful gift from the past."

Montblanc's voice began to waver and flutter as he finished his story. As I silently looked at him, my eyes now somewhat adjusted to the dark, I noticed something just barely visible under the finite light, something that I thought was impossible. A tear was falling from his eye.

This was the first and only time I have ever seen him cry and I was immediately discomforted by the sight. Partially because of the subversion of my established expectations, but more so because of the impact I knew this was going to have on the dynamic between us. How was I supposed to cope with this new information? As the Master stood before me in brazen vulnerability I felt in myself an uneasy power, as if I had just picked up a handgun that I still had no idea how to fire.

I chose to stay quiet. After taking a moment to wipe away the renegade tear from his face, Maxime continued his verbal ruminations, though his current emotional state caused a small lapse in the rhythmic cadence and excessive eloquence that he normally displayed, prompting the virtuoso rhetorician to speak quite plainly.

"About seven years ago I found myself in the interior of British Columbia for an event with the Party. Very close once again to those teal-tinged trees where two sprouting souls were once laid bare. On the final night I decided to forgo the haughtiness of the fundraising dinner, this at a time when my absence could have gone largely unnoticed, endeavoring instead to act on the opportunity to revisit the shrine of my burgeoning fecundity. That place, unfindable except by those who would already know where to find it. That place where she and I, shielded under dense branches, drew out and dwelt upon the strange viscus we both seemed to share. How different would those trees appear through the eyes of a man now as weathered as I?

"But that question was to remain unanswered.

"The trees were gone. Cut down and carried away. And in their place? A parking lot. A parking lot I could never envision being full. A dread crawled its way up through my body as I realized that my memories were now the only reference point I had left. The wheel of modernization always turns, this I know and embrace, for it has made me my fortune, but for first time I felt as if the wheel had dragged itself across my chest in a petty effort of karmic realignment. There was no doubt a pain to be felt, though I also recognized the futility of lingering on it. Change and decay are inevitabilities—this I was able to acknowledge without further consideration. Until tonight. Until the harbingers of the past decided to collect on my sins. And make no mistake, Lawrence, my guilt is unquestionable and I deserve everything that's sure to come my way. But that that is my burden alone. Those trees didn't do anything wrong, did they? Collateral damage caught in the wake of my rise, but they didn't do anything wrong. And neither did she . . ."

It sounds again like Montblanc is about to start weeping. He sits himself on the end of my bed and holds his face in his hands. I don't know what to say to him and I'm still not entirely sure what he's just said to me. I see now that he has removed his left hand from his face and it seems to be repeatedly squeezing something that isn't there, a lost gesture, a secret handshake. Acting on sympathetic intuition I get out of the bed and take a seat next to him. A short beat passes and I gauchely put one arm around him. To my surprise he leans his body toward mine, accepting my unpolished attempt at embrace. Instinctually I put my other arm around him and he buries his face in my chest. And now I am holding this lumbering beast of a man in both my arms like a parent holding their child. As I hold the man— the probable future Prime Minister—and comfort him from a bad dream that he just had, I realize the absurdity of my current position and almost let out a small chuckle. I catch myself, and instead look again toward the electronic clock and its still-stalwart LED lights of order. 3:27 am. What a time to be alive. And just like that, in a span of no more than ten minutes, I learned something about my host. Something incredibly important.

The robe was made of fleece.

## 41

## Propinquity

QUESTIONS ABOUND REGARDING the mental stability of my host. Why do I get the feeling that I am being shouted at through a movie screen by nervous viewers begging me to get out of the house before it's too late? Until now I've been rolling with the spontaneity of this whole experience in a very uncharacteristic way, first and foremost as a means of eventually securing a cheque with a truly alleviating number of zeros written just to the right of my name, and second, as a meager but honest attempt to break out of what the deluded disciples of Dionysus would refer to as 'my shell.' I've never been one to jump into unfamiliar bodies of water without first measuring the exact distance to the bottom and taking role call of all the beasties and fanged fish lurking in the murky depths. But here I am. In the service and space of a man whose emotional state is unpredictable and whose mental wellness is questionable. My efforts to track some sort of pattern in his behaviour and moods have so far been folly, and as such, I'm willing to open the floor to bets.

Come on, who wants to put their money down on what we will see tonight? Will he come in guns blazing, berating me with a torrent of well-worded insults right out of the gate? Will he be strictly business and keep our discussion brief and related purely to the book? Maybe he'll remember another tree from his youth that got cut down and start crying again? Christ, I sure as hell hope not. Well? Any takers? Side bets on whether or not he will belittle me for having a speech impediment. Maybe tonight is the night he finally makes the proposition that we go to bed together? Or maybe he will attack me physically and I'll be forced to defend myself against a man six inches taller and sixty pounds

heavier than me? Your guess is as good as mine. Empathetic readers, and bless your hearts, might be wondering why I endure the
unscripted chaos that I do. Unfortunately, I don't have a good
answer for that, though I do see it as a stamina test of sorts. If I
can put in my time, finish the book, and manage to walk out of
here after a job well done, I will have made per$onal growth and
reached a new level of exi$tential $atisfaction. And isn't that really what life is all about?

Now, concerning Montblanc . . .

At an improper sideways glance, you might think that the
two of us were compatible figures, both desperately clinging
on to the last remaining seed as if its sprouting and our validation were untenably entwined. Clinging on, yes. Squeezing
out the life, especially yes. Let that then be our grand irony,
with our swollen iron glands and our tandem gridiron dance of
ire, fire and sand. In your mind I'll ask that you let that mis-
conceived miscarriage end as all ought to, for I'm finding with
each passing day the outlooks of myself and Mr. Emmy, our
perpetually polite parliamentarian, to be oceans apart. Still, I
find myself in an unexpected state of reverence, bordering on
awe, as I am made witness to the circumstances that meticulously mixed the martini of a man I have been endeavored to
elucidate in way that is palatable for the mouth-breathing public. Hey, careful now. Don't insult the audience like that.
That's no way to win friends and influence people. Montblanc
speaks in a way that I wish I could. That alone comprises the
list of his traits that I would want to share. Still, I feel blessed
in my opportunity to transmute his life onto paper, partially
because I also get to learn about the nuances of his life that
won't make it to print.

But an uneasiness looms within me. This man, composed
equally of marvelousness and madness, has a high likelihood of
becoming the elected leader of this country. That is a fence I
don't know which side to stand on. Maybe all great leaders have
had the subtle hands of lunacy laid upon them at some point?
After all, I've heard world leaders give speeches, I've read their
words, I've seen the images they project, but I've never person-

ally known any of them. Maybe behind closed doors they're all a little different. Maybe they're all a little Monty...

I choose to believe this for now. I have to. Lest the fear of this force unleashed partially by my hand embrace me in its paralyzing arms.

# 42

## PYROCLASTICS

THE ERUPTION HAPPENED as the morning sun was attempting the horizon, the day's first light denied as a concoction of smoke and rock burst from the caldera obscuring the entirety of the sky's canvas. A thick ash blanketed the jungle suffocating flora and fauna alike as a lifeless silence fell around the base of the burning mountain. From the cataclysmic sludge the Boy struggled to emerge and draw first breath.

Following his first steps the Boy's feet turned tough as boiled leather but a mighty hunger remained. He walked naked across the scorched jungle floor on some impulse of nourishment. He found nothing worth eating until he had nearly exited the area of immediate destruction. On the ground lay an okapi half-burnt but still alive and immobilized under the nearly hardened magma. The creature wheezed as its lame body remain trapped and broken. The Boy descended upon this gift, biting through the thick skin of its neck and sucking its blood through his teeth. The okapi's eyes remained open and wide as the Boy eventually chewed through the trachea. The creature died soon after and the Boy ate until he could no longer, his face dotted with hardened and hardening blood. The Boy stood over the corpse and wiped the blood from his hands onto his lean and muscular abdomen. He noticed the red lines on his stomach left by his fingers and proceeded to cover the entirety of his chest with the seemingly endless supply of searing crimson at his feet. With his thumbs he scooped out the creature's eyes and taking one in either hand collided them hard and fast against his chest.

The Boy ran. He ran naked and fast, his legs never stiffening, his lungs never failing him. Sweat fell from his brow mixing with the dried blood on his face, landing salty atop his tongue hung loose out his mouth. He ran deep into the thick of the jungle still lush and untouched by the morning's eruption. His feet landed indiscriminately on insects and animal scat. He bound over branches and fallen trees. He was dexterous enough to snatch mosquitos out of the air midstride and shove them into his mouth, their spindly legs occasionally catching between his sharp teeth. And he ran on like thunder crashing until he came across a small clearing.

An infant gorilla scarcely taller than the grass was walking clumsy as his mother watched on nearby. The Boy's run shifted to a cautious walk as he approached the infant primate with a new curiosity. As the distance between them closed the infant's mother with no wasted movement set to protecting her child from the upright stranger. With a screech the mother sprinted toward the Boy who swiftly jumped and rolled to evade her charge. The Boy darted his head in all directions looking for any advantage he might use against his oversized opponent. The mother charged again and again the Boy with sonic reflexes dodged the attack. He then noticed the skeletal remains of some animal long departed. The bones had been stripped clean of all protein and strewn about the clearing save for a small pile that the Boy quickly bound toward. The mother had regrouped with her baby and continued to screech at the Boy who had now picked up a femur bone slightly shorter than his own arm. Holding the bone at its base with both hands the Boy slowly walked toward mother and child. With another harrowing shriek the mother once again charged the Boy who in one fluid motion sidestepped the charge while bringing down the bone atop the gorilla's skull with force enough to break his improvised weapon in half. The Boy's hands rang with the force of the impact as he used the half he was still holding, its ends now jagged where it had been split, to stab the dazed mother in the face several times over. Once the beast had fallen defenseless to the ground, its eyes and face now lost, the Boy recovered the other half of the bone and with one half in each hand proceeded to bludgeon the mother's skull in a flurry of up-and-down blows as if he were trying to puncture the skin of some tribal drum.

The mother lay dead on her stomach with her thoughts exposed and littered atop the grass. The Boy noticed her lifeless rump pointed upward in a manner he found inviting. He relieved himself on the corpse and wiped his member on its fur as the infant watched on. In the infant's eyes the Boy saw a vulnerability. He picked up the infant by its neck, leaned back far, and hurled it deep into the woods where he could no longer see or be seen by its vulnerable and accusing eyes.

The Boy ran on, his legs unspent and furiously pumping. He stopped briefly to release excrement, some of which landed on his calf and clung to the hair of his legs. He ran on and by the time the sun had started its nightly withdrawal the volcano from which he spawned seemed a fading landmark in the distance. It grew dark and his eyes adjusted quickly. He stopped running and felt pangs of hunger in his stomach. He picked an indiscernible lump out of his matted hair and ate it though this did little to satiate him. And then he saw the light from a flame nearby.

The Boy was born of fire from the Earth's core and so would the fire always attract him. He walked slow toward the source of the flame and as it grew nearer, he saw the structures made of wood and crafted with expertise and care. He noticed five of these structures build in a circular fashion and in the middle of this circle the fire burned tall. The Boy could see no others and approached cautiously, but the inhabitants of the settlement had heard whispers from the jungle and had prepared for the Boy's arrival. Just as he was to emerge from the brush and breach the perimeter of the settlement, his right foot was snared tightly by a rope that lay obscured on the ground and he was lifted partially into the air by a spring noose mechanism that he did not understand. As he dangled the Boy began thrashing about to free himself creating great noise in the process. He heard vocalizations from the nearby structures which exacerbated his panic. Through the muscles of his core he brought his mouth to his dangling ankle in an impressive display of flexibility and began to gnaw at the rope. The inhabitants of the settlement continued to muster and soon a group of four set out to approach their catch. They approached carefully by the light of a solitary torch, but when they arrived the Boy was gone and had left no trace save for the broken rope he had chewed through.

The Boy ran on through the night rejuvenated by the fear of his near capture. He ate leaves and other forage when he could find it but he was pained with cravings of flesh. He was growing fast. His naked body was bruised and bloodied and filthy but still he ran. He was born of rock and flame. He left the trees behind and came across a mountain. He was ejaculated from the Earth in a burst of destruction. He climbed the mountain. He moves on impulse. He is the king of all he surveys. At the top of the mountain he sees skyscrapers and highways in the distance. He urinates on his feet. His feet are tough as boiled leather. He descends on the metropolis. He is the son of the Earth. They were not ready for him. Lava courses through his veins. It was rapturous and despaired. He is the Boy.

He is the Man.

# 43

## POLTOPHAGY

It SHOULD GO without saying that I've never been accused of talking too much. Thinking too much? Now that's a much more valid criticism. I realize that my role here is to act as a buffer between Montblanc and all of you out there in the real world, but lately I've been wondering if I could be subtler about it. For instance, M asked me to help him prepare dinner tonight. On the surface this started as an uneventful affair that resulted in what I thought was a good meal, but beneath every action subtext festered and seethed, each moment acting as a potential power play. Or maybe that's just me overinterpreting things as you know I do. What if I were to let you decide? I submit to the jury the mostly complete transcript of tonight's conversation with M in the kitchen. I've omitted all my responses, thoughts, and interpretations, leaving only the words of the Big Man himself. Based on this evidence I'll allow you to decide how much of my guidance you think is necessary moving forward.

★★★

Thank you, Lawrence. That we may share in both the process and the results of this labour will surely enhance what nourishment soon follows. Shall we begin? Tonight's entrée is a Hawaiian pineapple chicken which we will serve alongside a pilaf of wild rice and green beans. Admittedly this dish is perhaps a touch pedestrian, but I would ask you withhold any reservations you may have until your first taste comes to pass. What traces of pulchritude lay dormant in such simplicities may be overlooked by those of haughtier predispositions, but will never become imperceptible to us my dear friend.

*Alors,* before we begin I would kindly ask you to wash your hands. It's not that I worry where they have been, my concern rests with where they are headed. Yes, a rich lather, that's the way, and the pleasing scent of hibiscus rewards our diligence. Very good. Now if you agree I will assume the role of saucier, not because I doubt your capacities, but because I need you to prepare the pineapple. Inside that brown bag you will find it. No, Lawrence, the other bag. And *voilà,* there it is. Some may lay claim that using canned pineapple will suffice for this dish but I won't allow it, for the entirety of your existence may become preprocessed should you submit to the enfeebling influence of convenience. Have you ever peeled and cored a pineapple before? Ah, well there is a first time for everything. See the knife block there? The one in the middle, the chef's knife, that's the one you'll want to use for this. Yes, take off the top and remove the outer layer but do not be too bold with your cuts, the outer layer is thin. Remarkable fruits, wouldn't you say? The spiny and resilient exterior conceals a true and succulent form with a hint of tartness, but venture too far inward and be met again with a hardened core inedible to most and often discarded without second thought. Now what does that remind you of? Forgive me, a kitchen requires ordered instruction and quantifiability and is hardly the place to explore such metaphors, I'll allow you to prepare the pineapple undisturbed and with due attention.

Finished then? Very nice, Lawrence, this will do splendidly. Next is the chicken, you will find it in the refrigerator. I hope you have fostered an appetite because we will be using all of it. It can be sliced with the very same knife. I am not deaf to the plights of the vegetarians and I'll not do you the discourtesy of attempting to justify or exonerate myself from any of the utilitarian or existential perspectives available. Swift winds will carry what has not been fastened to the ground, but who in these circumstances would lay blame on the weather in lieu of their own lack of foresight? And if that is what you truly believe, then for what reason would I have to doubt that claim? And concerning the flesh sat currently under your fingertips? At times I perceive your cleverness as a crutch. What would you make of a person whose first response to any line of questioning or conversation is cleverness? Many of us have clever thoughts. So too do many of us have the capability to reserve voicing such thoughts at times when they have nothing to contribute. Now see to the chicken, sliced thin please.

Now the pineapple can go on top and we can cover the lot of it with the sauce. Care to do the honours? Yes, use it all, now is not the time for reticence, let not a naked mark remain. Into the oven with it. And then we wait. We will start the rice and the beans shortly, but we mustn't rush. You of all people know the folly of making decisions too brashly I'm sure. I say it because the stock of your life's accomplishments may be more readily counted than those of this very kitchen. Your silence betrays you. I have invited you to cook at my side as an equal but should you desire me to speak with a more rigid tongue I worry this arrangement may then be compromised. Do not misconstrue my purpose, dear Lawrence, I've no intentions of acting as a surrogate to any of the coaches, teachers, or parental figures of your past. I speak to you plain out of respect, you might consider gauging your reactions thusly. What's that tired idiom? If you can't handle the heat, get out of the kitchen. Seems particularly apt given the circumstances, no? The water is boiling, take care of those beans, would you?

Now the plating and presentation of the dish is as important as the preparation itself so we must ensure that we do this with the utmost of care. Yes, I am aware that only you and I are indulging. Are you suggesting the presentation becomes less important because of this? If you are unwilling to show pride in matters of isolation how can you expect to shine bright amid the world's darkness? And now the chicken can be placed directly atop the rice. Yes, wonderful Lawrence, just as so. If you would be so kind as to bring those lovely dishes to the table, I will excuse myself for a moment to fetch an appropriate wine to accompany our dinner.

Thank you once again for your aid in preparing dinner. Is it to your liking? Glad to hear it.

For shared meals are not bound by the same rigidity, would-
n't you say? Don't answer that. Just keep eating. Ingest the
proteins and nutrients and grow strong and large. You are too
petite to be mistaken for my son. Mann. Your surname is of
Germanic origin, no? I would have expected a better return
based on your stock. They are a people predisposed to the clot-
ting of their blood. I recall a man I met in Germany, he fancied
himself an architect but what he truly wanted was to make a lasting mark on the world. Red-faced and full of tequila he told me
he was going to build a fantastic bridge of concrete across the
Atlantic Ocean. From New York to Quimper, a multinational
arrangement, but built exclusively by Germans, he was very clear
to that point. He insisted that he had financial and political support and that I would be driving across this bridge within a dozen
years. I no longer recall that man's name. In truth I never bothered to commit it to memory in the first place. A year after our
meeting I had my people track him down, for I was curious to
see what progress he had made on his life's work. As it happens
he was already dead. Complications resulting from a blood clot.
Probably for the better, for his idea was ludicrous and not at all
grounded in reality. I told him as much when he explained it to
me but his resolve remained unshaken. The delusional fool sincerely believed his ridiculous bridge would be built and that it
would bear his name and remain a testament to his skill and
ambition long after he was gone. The financial and political support he claimed to have collected were just additional facets of
this fantasy. That man died from clotted blood. His name remains
unknown by all save for the unimportant few by necessity who
now make dismal attempts at keeping it alive at dinner tables
much like this one. But when they speak, the sound of his name
does not reverberate and echo throughout their halls. It's spoken
as a faint whisper, growing softer like a flame circling wick's end.
Something you might consider, Mann. Now finish your plate,
more food awaits you. Grow strong and grow large.

Although it is not just his name that eludes me. I know it's
not becoming to admit, but I must confess that it makes me so
angry, at times unbearably so. I feel a hole forming behind my

skull and memories drip through it like a leaking faucet. It gets hot and I feel tight in my skin when I acknowledge what is lost and what is slipping. I was building to a point and now it has escaped me. Leave the table. Yes, leave your plate, leave the table, leave the room, just leave. Do not tempt my temper, Lawrence, dinner is over. Just pick yourself up and leave. You've had your fill and your plate is empty. Dinner is over. This is over. Never mind the dishes, I'll look after them. Now for the last time vacate this room before I'm inclined to fall victim to the wiles of these crones whispering rage in my ears. We speak no more of this.

★★★

And then I left the room and returned to my bedroom in the basement. And so ends dinner with Maxime Montblanc, free of any interjections or commentary on my part. Well, was it more or less clarifying without my internal monologue? About half a minute after heading downstairs I hear a plate being smashed against the tiles of the kitchen floor. Maybe he dropped it by accident? Either way I suppose that's not for me to say.

# 44

## Prosaicness

Wouldn't it be wild if it turned out that Montblanc was just a figment of my imagination the entire time?

# 45

## PROSITS

I SLEPT IN late this morning. But I'm a good worker ant and I can pull my own weight several times over. I would blame pain or anger but you can't explicitly state any of these things without instantly becoming a parody of them. No value in unsophisticated musings. Sometimes I stay quiet because I don't want to struggle through words, but mostly I stay quiet because I can't think of anything meaningful to say. Instead I'll let Montblanc's meticulously maintained muniments speak for themselves while I do my best to fill in the gaps between the hotel receipts, the cryptic notes scribbled onto branded notepaper, and the unsigned letters of unfamiliar penmanship.

***

The glassy month of December in the year 2000. Just shy of two weeks since Montblanc won his seat in the Canadian Parliament for the first time. The receipt from the Fairmont Hotel Vancouver specifies that he spent one night in room 1023. And while he was indeed within the hotel's walls that night, the bed in room 1023 was never laid upon.

In the lobby a three-piece band played at a reserved volume while Montblanc spoke to the receptionist and arranged to have his suitcase brought to his room on the tenth floor. He didn't ascend himself. He instead sat in trepidation in the lobby under the pretense of listening to the band. He might have considered running to the roof where the air was thin. He might have considered asking the band if he could sit in on the keys for a few songs. Neatly folded and stored in his back pocket was the unsigned letter containing the instructions for the meeting that was about to occur. It was written purple with the ambiguity he normally might have detested and he kept it on his person despite having memorized its contents. In the brief silence before the band started their next song Montblanc lifted himself heavily from the lobby furnishings, gave a nod of appreciation to the musicians, and entered the waiting elevator.

Montblanc walked the quiet halls of the eighth floor looking for the room with the slightly opened door as the letter instructed. It was early in the evening and none of the rooms he passed hinted at any signs of inhabitants. A part of him might have been hoping that he never found that door. But he did. He stood outside it for a moment before he slowly pushed it open with an untypical meekness, and as his view of the room's interior expanded he saw her sitting at the table beside the window with curtains drawn.

"You weren't waiting long, I hope."

"No, I was just watching a history show on TV. I asked the receptionist to call me when you arrived so I could get into position at the table here. Not bad, huh?"

"Very thespian indeed. Much in line with the convoluted method with which you brought me here."

"You're not complaining are you, Maxime?"

"Never. This history program, what was it about?"

"The War of 1812. The role of Tecumseh specifically. He was quite the leader, you know. Seems you both have that in common."

"Thank you. But I'm afraid I don't see the comparison."

"Still, congratulations either way. I suspect this new job will be keeping you quite busy?"

"No more than usual, though it will be different to be sure."

"Well, I'm proud of you, Max. But then, we aren't here to talk about that, are we?"

"We are not."

"I'd prefer if we didn't need to talk about anything."

"Might be best to just say it plain. If this is indeed to be our last night together I'd rather we not linger any longer than we need to on this unpleasantness."

"Unpleasantness. That's a word for it, I suppose."

"So, it's the uterus then?"

"The endometrium more specifically."

"And?"

"Remember that thing you wrote about summer skies and the moon bearing witness?"

"It was worded more elegantly than that as I recall."

"Well I don't think I'll be seeing any more summer skies."

"What of your husband?"

"He's wanted kids for a long time. I wouldn't dream of taking that away from him, even if he can't think that far ahead just yet. But let's talk about something else. What about you?"

"What about me?"

"Have you looked into that . . . unpleasantness with your dad?"

★★★

"Well, Maxime, I guess this is really it for us then."

"I suppose so."

"Then I want you. I want you one last time."

"Is that . . . Are you so sure that's a good idea?"

"I don't think that matters at this point. This may well be my last chance, and not just with you."

"That certainly introduces some pressure."

"*Mon Dieu!* You poor thing! Now come here, there'll be plenty of time to mope afterwards."

"How well you know me."

"Now be gentle, Maxime. You'll need to be gentle."

# 46

## PARAGONS

WITH MASTER MONTBLANC in Ottawa for the next few days and with thoughts of constraint and lost agency starting to taunt my sedentary situation, I decided to play a little hooky. Yes, I will hold for applause. Cherish me as the pillar of the human condition. But what of the rest? Cooped up in these environs I felt myself becoming detached. What life is mine? Hunched over a desk all day, piecing together the life story of a man who has all but made a prisoner out of me? Aristotle reminds us that humans are social animals, and for me to re-establish the required link with my mammalian brethren I must once again dive headfirst into the cultural zeitgeist, the mana of humanity, the—ah, fuck it, what I'm trying to say is that I bailed on work today to go see a movie.

The theatre was nearly empty when I arrived after walking nearly an hour from M's castle. Apparently not the hottest ticket in town at 3:15 on a Wednesday afternoon. So much for surrounding myself with people. That's okay, the film itself is sure to provide me easy access to the full spectrum of human emotion. I took a seat in the middle of an empty aisle. That is, I *chose* a seat in the middle of an empty aisle. A few others trickled in as I fervently watched the pre-show advertisements. Sell me the world. Sell me a place to belong. Sell me my own seat in the middle of an empty aisle. I notice that I'm the only one sitting by myself. I hope that I am not responsible for any feelings of empathy. We are all friends in this dark room. We are all sharing our quest for the human condition. We are all in this together. I will never leave any of you.

Time now for our feature presentation.

I know nothing of the film other than that it's a sequel to a movie about superheroes. As I submit to losing myself in the narrative I find that occasional snippets of dialogue ricochet within my head longer than they were probably intended to, threatening my immersion, and indeed, the very mission itself.

*As you know, the Totality Crystal has been safe in Washington since the battle with Dreadnought four years ago.*

If we already know this then why say it? Shameless exposition without any trace of subtlety or tact. Hold on. Relax. Don't start getting critical yet, the movie just started. Remember why you're here, you can let this one go.

*Meet Dr. Ophelia Everett, she's in charge of the laboratory.*

Let me guess—she falls in love with the protagonist? And why would they name her Ophelia? Already this story could generously be described as trite and now they want to drag old Billy through it?

*If that seal is broken it would unleash a power that could demolish any army on Earth. It wouldn't be a battle—it would be a slaughter.*

Oh my. That sure was some powerful and convincing language and the stakes certainly seem high this time around. I wonder how our heroes will ever be able to defeat such an enemy.

*This specialized suit will allow you to tap into powers you didn't even know you had.*

I can't do it. I'm sinking. I'm caught in a malignant maelstrom of spite and frustration, delivered to you now, unfiltered and unrefined so that some good may yet come from this failed experiment:

Heroes assemble and show me the meaning of virtue. Go on adventures I could never have, speak dialogue I could never say. I can see it all. I see the close-up shots of the misty-eyed female lead. I see the crew spraying her eyes in-between takes. I see the swelling minor key of the soundtrack, invisibly manipulating my emotions. I see them stumble through the predictable plot. I see the three act formula in place. I see the computer-generated explosions obstructing every inch of the frame. I see the lightning-fast cuts disorienting my senses and trapping me in the action. I see the syringe filled with pathos being injected into my eyelids. I see the steps that were taken to get to this point, and yet I can't bring myself to follow them. I have no business being here. These people want justice, catharsis, and the triumph of good over evil served up in an easily digestible two-hour meal. They aren't my friends. I can't speak their language. The film is reaching its emotional climax now and as it does I feel my life as a profane and wasted thing. With the days dropping slowly but noticeably audible like the leaking roof gradually filling the spare cast-iron pot (the one I never use), I wonder how much time remains before a meniscus is formed, that being the final warning sign of the inevitable overflow. 'No', as obsessive thoughts form around this ignominious end. My life to be represented by a few drops of escaped water, so easily wiped up and forgotten? I want to be a stain on the floor, something that the combination of elbow grease, home remedies, and brand name promises would not be able to remove.

Something unexpected now happens. As the film draws to a close I become wholly engrossed in the narrative. These heroes are on the brink of defeat, but they find the strength within them to resolve and carry on. It's so life-affirmingly beautiful. With their combined efforts they finally defeat the villain and I feel a grand release. A tear is forming behind my right eye as this inspiring story gently guides me through its dénouement. Fade to black, roll credits. For a split second I swear I can see my name on the black background as a cover version of a popular song from the 1980s begins to play. People have started getting out of their seats and slowly shuffling toward the exit and the blinding sun waiting beyond the cinema doors. But I stay in my seat in the middle of an empty aisle as one-by-one the room empties. I read every name that scrolls across the screen and soon I am the last one there. The lights come on. I wipe away the tear that almost escaped. My reintegration is complete.

You may now cherish me as the pillar of the human condition.

# 47

## PUTRESCENCE

AFTER LEAVING THE cinema, not content with the thought of surrendering the emerging evening to Montblanc's empty house, and still very much riding the waves of ethereal inspiration crashing against my standardly soundless shores, I decided to further tease the possibilities of spontaneity and keep this party goin'. What a mistake that was.

I'm sat at the bar of a local pub, waiting for something to save me. It's one of the few drinkeries on this street that has yet to be bought out by a chain and converted into their cookie-cutter parameters, and the relatively impressive amount of people here early on a Wednesday evening suggests that the owners might be able to avoid this fate. That's worth a toast. I've been nursing the same bottle of Coors, now my third, for about forty-five minutes, the label long since peeled off by nervous and unfocused hands. Though far from my favourite beer, Coors is the easiest for me to say, and I didn't want to burden the unignorably attractive bartender with my eternal struggle to pronounce *hefeweizen*. No, I'll stay quiet. Just a man of few words, sitting at the bar by himself. Maybe she thinks there's something appealing about that? Maybe she'll want to know more about this mysterious and pensive stranger? Or maybe she sees losers like me every day. Stop. Don't go down that road. Not tonight. Tonight is all about experiencing the joys of civilization. The Penguins are playing the Rangers on the television that's mounted above the bar, and while I have no investment in either of those teams or the outcome of the game, I keep my eyes focused on the screen. If I can keep them there I don't have to worry about where they might end up.

When I arrived here an hour and a half ago I was under the delusion that sitting down at the bar and ordering a drink would be the magical password that ushered me into a night of jovial revelry and comradery with my fellow brothers and sisters, but instead I'm sitting by myself, drinking tepid beer that I don't really like, watching a hockey game that I don't care about, trying to catch the eye of a woman who probably just wants me to pay up and leave. Yeah, I'm a real rock star. Someday I'll be the one who's paying an idealistic young writer to document the escapades of my electrifying life. But for now, I think I'll go check out the bathroom. I don't really have to go, but maybe someone will stop me on the walk over and invite me to their table. It could happen.

Of course it didn't, and now I find myself sitting in a bathroom stall, pants still on, in a truly pathetic attempt to kill some time before I return back to my seat. Maybe they will have moved it to the corner and provided a dunce cap for me by now? Helping me pass the time are the brave men who came before me, those heroic souls who had the courtesy to scribble messages all over the walls of this stall. I share with you now some of the more elegant examples.

*Help it smells*

I feel for you, brother, but we've all got problems. Here in the loo, the great leveler, all men are made equal. Here the great taboos unite us all. I can't do much, but I'll keep you in my thoughts and pray that the white flowers of vanilla accompany the precious moments of your future.

*Jesus fucks*

This reminds me—while in university I met a girl who claimed to be sexually attracted to Jesus—something she apparently only told people she really trusted. She said it was something about his eyes, and the way that they were sad, but at the same time warm and inviting. She told me that her fantasy would be to lay him down, climb on top of his slender body, and show him the wonders of human sin. One sentence in particular has always stuck with me, a button permanently placed on the soundboard of my memories. 'He wouldn't last a minute, but we would cherish every second.' I wonder what it is about my own eyes, neither sad nor warm, that lead people to trust me.

*Why do so many people shit with pens?*

Actually a very apt inquiry. These are the things we tend not to think about. Ours is a society focused on the final product, not the processes of making said product. Unless the final product happens to be the soon-to-be Prime Minister.

*SPEAK ENGLISH*

Nice to see that myopic ethnocentric sentiments exist near the shitter where they belong.

*Josies cunt*

Forgiving the lack of a possessive apostrophe, who is Josie? Does she know that she is the muse of this porcelain-pot poet? The legatee of this literary latrine laureate's loyalty? Does she know that her cunt is of concern to this commode commentator, this lavatory lecturer? Is she aware that *her* facilities are the focal point of the walls of *these* facilities? Josie, I may never meet you, but now that I've become acquainted with your reputation, I long to know if this bard of the boy's room ever had his affections requited.

*There are no diamonds in the mine.*

A cryptic comment on constipation perhaps? This sounds so familiar, but I can't quite put my finger on where I might've heard it before . . .

*Treat sluts like sluts*

You know, I've never actually seen a glory hole in real life before. I'm sure they exist somewhere, just probably not in the types of places I would normally visit. In these environs it is difficult not to shed fastidiousness and libidinous modesty—still, my approach would likely be one of whimsy and nothing more. I'm something of a coward in that regard. Might explain why I'm thirty years old and hiding in a bathroom stall.

*Women have dicks too!*

Your guess is as good as mine on this one.

*Power without love is a dangerous thing.*

Hold on a minute. How did unexpectedly profound words find themselves here of all places? More importantly, how did *I* find myself here? The mood in this men's room shifts. What lost perseverance beckons me back to task? Would Montblanc find peace in the thought of me pretending to be the sarcastic king of this particular partition when he has scheduled my talents elsewhere? Do I owe allegiance to the loveless power shaping my days? I sit here having found futility in the promises of freedom and now I yearn for the safety of my cell once again. I felt better watching my warden's long arm dangle the cell keys from Ottawa, leaving me to the happy endings of daydreams.

That's it. If I leave now I can still get a good chunk of work done. Let today's failed experiment serve as a reminder to the grim possibilities that arise from petulant attempts at jollity. Find my brain floating in formaldehyde, lob the beach ball toward it, expect more gesticulation from it than from me. I am the world champion of servility. I write the annals, so I ought to know that there's no mention of me to be found within them. I have a $13.50 bar tab. I will leave a $20 bill. God Save the Queen. And while He is doing that, I have a job to do.

It's time to shit or get off this pot.

## 48

## PALISADES

As I FLEE the bar I'm met with twilight outside. The usual evening crowd hasn't even arrived yet and I'm already running home with my head pointed to the ground. 'Home', he says, as if that were at all the correct word to use. It would be a ten-minute cab ride back to *la maison de Montblanc,* but oddly this day of repeated failures has yet to take the last bit of wind from my idiomatic sails. I chose instead to walk, banking on the hope that something will happen on the way back that can justify leaving in the first place.

Montblanc's neighbourhood is lifeless on this Wednesday evening and so I pretend that the sidewalk is a red carpet that was rolled out for me personally. That façade fades as I'm overcome with the urge to enter each house that I pass. In lieu of my dejectedness and the day's failures I muse instead on the endless possibilities each house offers. I want to go inside every room. I want to know what's stored in the boxes in the basements. I want to see the art hung on every wall. I want to discover what secrets are being incautiously kept in bedside tables. Instead all I get are brief glimpses into lives I could never inhabit. A few seconds to pass by each dwelling and collect as much information as I can. Through a kitchen window I see a spice rack, and though I can't distinguish any of them, I wonder how they might be used to cook a meal for me. A meal where I meet her parents. A meal where a deal is made. Next house. Through a basement window I see a flag with the Ottawa Senators logo on it. That same house has a basketball hoop in the driveway. Next house. I notice the inhabitants are watching the CBC on a colossal TV screen. I wonder if they were excited when they bought it. I wonder if anyone raised concerns.

Maybe I'll be saved yet. Maybe someone will drive by and invite me to come home with them. These are thoughts pulled like levers in the utmost of sincerity by gamblers chasing their losses. Next house. I see a barbeque on the patio. Wooden fences separate each yard. Fences block everything that I was never meant to see.

Coming across an elementary school now and I fixate on the playground on the other side of a chain link fence. Every house thus far has been a denial, but this, well this is an opportunity to finally assert my humanity. Less than a minute later I'm sat on a swing set that I am far too big for, retracing the steps that brought me to this pathetic moment in time.

It was from a need to be heard. It still is. Like the bowels of houses recently passed my internal grievances remain unelucidated to those beyond the fence. Pity has been an unwelcome companion, doggedly following me around ever since my voice was first stolen and it remains with me still. I see it in the faces of everyone who is subjected to my fractured words. But pity can never match what empathy is able to accomplish. I would happily explain the difference if only the words could come out. I would happily write the difference if only my words weren't already bought and owned. They don't know what it's like. And now I'm drifting dangerously close to self-pity—infinitely worse. But how did I get here?

It's the swing set I'm sitting on and the prepubescent memories it excavates. It's the empty playground. It's the twilight. It's the houses and their secrets I will never know. It's the three beers in my stomach. It's the empty and unmade bed I'm putting off returning to. It's my voice and my words, both robbed from me. It's the pity I don't want but know that I deserve. It's more than that. It's the clandestine thoughts that can never be expressed. It's the crass graffiti in a men's room stall that will be read more than my words ever will. It's the cold chains in my hands. It's the winds from nearby Lake Ontario unwelcomingly caressing my cheeks. It's the teenage couple that sat on this swing set while murmuring premature promises. It's the pointless, meandering journey I've taken you on and the guilt I feel for wasting your time. It's the safety of familiarity. It's the familiarity of safety. It's the rust on Leonard Cohen's low E string. It's the publisher's rejection letters that I keep in a binder with my high school report cards. It's the asseveration that I meekly offer at the shrine of Tenjin. It's the predictability of the three-act structure that I've strained myself to eschew. It's the ladybug landed on my knee that I haven't the zeal to flick off. It's the faint flame in the hearth.

It's the faint flame in the hearth . . . And I think it's coming from Montblanc's house.

I don't know why I can't just stay down for the count. Where are these last droplets of vitality falling from? It doesn't matter, I suppose. They compel me off this swing set and toward the house where my alleged purpose currently resides. Not far away now. As I continue the journey I pass several more houses, though this time I'm not concerned with stealing quick glimpses inside, instead I'm trying to remember exactly what it was that Montblanc said to me when I first arrived. Among the ground rules that were established were the banal—I could come and go as I pleased, I could help myself to whatever food I wanted—but also the curious.

'Under no circumstances are you to venture to the top floor.'

Right. That was it. I didn't argue it or even question it at the time. The top floor is where his bedroom is. He needs his privacy and as his employee I was expected to respect that. It made sense. Besides, I had plenty of room and resources to myself. In addition to his guest bedroom he had essentially granted me the entire basement and ground level to use as an office for writing. I had no reason to explore the top level.

But I'm not about to leave this miserable mess of a day empty-handed.

As I walk up the long driveway to M's front door, I feel the sweat that has formed on my shoulders, due in part to my brisk walk through this warm summer night, but more so to the nervousness I felt for the rule that I had already in my mind broken. Using the spare key entrusted to me I unlock the front door and already my mind is working overtime to rationalize my decision.

To know the man, to write about the man with any degree of authority, I must know his secrets. I open the door and unlace my Chucks. They look somewhat puerile next to Montblanc's panoply of posh pedial prisons. This isn't an invasion of privacy or a breach of trust. This is research. Nothing more. I make my way to the staircase and my right foot lands on top of the first step for the first time. He said near the beginning that I needed to know him complete. I am the artist. I need to be able to follow the trail that the muse presents. I climb the stairs. As I do I issue myself a compromise—just his bedroom, nothing else. That way I can sleep soundly on this excursion being entirely work-related. The last room on the right. Somehow I already know that's where it is. During my approach I notice several framed photographs hanging in the hallway. In one of them I see an attractive man standing on a rock overlooking a body of water. I know that it's not Max, but I don't break my stride long enough to pick up any other details. The last room on the right. I take a deep breath. I pause for the camera and for the audience. This would be a good time to cut to a commercial. I shake my head. I open the door.

I've heard that following the tragedy of a child's demise, parents will often maintain their bedrooms as a type of static shrine that remains unchanged throughout time. This was my first thought as I enter Montblanc's chamber. I can't ignore the remnants of a wife still here. The flowers on the mirrored desk, once as purple as my prose, have wilted and deceased. The room emits a femininity that is both pleasant and offsetting. After standing still for a moment I get to work. I check the drawer directly under the fading flowers and find the handgun, nestled on top a pile of incongruent fabrics and coloured construction paper. I'm afraid to touch it. I've never held a gun in my life and while I know that it's most likely safe, I don't risk disturbing it. I turn my attention instead to the bed. It is blindingly white, as are the bedside tables on either end. On the bottom shelf of the left table I notice two books. Looking at their spines I see that one of these books I know quite well while the other is unmarked. I pick up and move the hardcopy version of *Restoring Conviction: The Hope and Faith of a Public Servant* to examine the book underneath it. There is no title on the cover. I open the book and am startled by my good fortune. There is handwriting inside—Montblanc's handwriting. This is it. Access to his private and uncensored thoughts. I turn to an arbitrary page and begin reading the man's private words.

I make it halfway through the page before I hear the door downstairs open.

## 49

## Psychopannychism

I SLEEP WHEN I'm scared—not a great evolutionary trait to have, is it?

As soon as I heard the door open my reflexes took over and within a second or two I had shut the book and returned it to its designated spot underneath my own. I bounded out the bedroom and made a dash down the hallway toward the stairs. I descended three steps before I locked eyes with the early-returned lord of the manor who was in the process of removing his shoes.

I sleep when I'm scared. It was earlier than my usual bedtime but I didn't want to process anything that had just happened. I only wanted sleep to overtake me. I only wanted to make it until the morning. I only wanted to turn these freshly burned revelations into shakeable dew.

When Montblanc saw my hasty exit from the forbidden floor his reaction was one of unsettling impassivity. He looked upon me for what felt like an eternity with no words and no change in expression. I was waiting for him to lose his temper. I was waiting for any type of reaction whatsoever. Wordlessly he finished removing his shoes as I slowly made my way down the remaining steps, the taciturn parliamentarian appearing larger with each gradual decrease in elevation.

I sleep when I'm scared. Consequences are best fought as faceless and unstoppable fiends in appropriate horrorscapes, not with words and dollars and other empirically quantifiable ammunitions. Lifeblood trickles down my calf, crusting on my leg hair.

After methodically placing his shoes on the nearby rack and his black pea coat on the nearby hanger, M picked up his luggage and started walking in my direction. I was still standing at the

base of the staircase, tense and mentally preparing for an impend-
ing punishment. With two steps he was standing directly in front
of me. He stood there for an uncomfortable beat or two and
then:

"Excuse me."

I stepped aside as he walked past me and up the stairs before
disappearing into what used to be unviolated territory.

I sleep when I'm scared. I feel that it's coming soon but still
not soon enough. This fear is multifaceted and intersectional. It
is partially measurable. What would the fallout be if he kicked me
off his book? But these fiduciary fears are now secondary to what
I think I remember seeing in that unmarked book upstairs. There
is no denying the words inside were his, and while I know I
remember some of the words that I saw, I can't be sure that the
images haven't been usurped by the frenzied architects of my
subconscious. As I slip into the remedial arms of sleep I'm
affronted by a bricolage of thoughts and phrases, some
attributable to what I saw in M's journal, some to myself, though
I no longer know where the dividing line is meant to exist.

★★★

*I just . . . I just like a lot. I'm numb to what I do not just to him.
A lot of nothing like what I just don't I mean I will die young enough.
That it is easy. To tell you nothing to be filthy to eat pussy was a single
sheet a little bigger. Listen. You'll naturally live with little until the air
is seen. Well if you'll come along who was looking at a sheet a shell a
diesel. Ideal finale she and she was here and tell him it had been a failing
weekend the journey said he's a lot more early he was a limb for the law
other than the sort of played well a lot.*

*Said yeah he's been doing. That. To me. Then. To bed with their
beloved passionate cogs in hand. Yes, he should eat. He then looks up
the national polls long study to look at the seller list and the legal
slimmest things like a living hell. Good chunk of the body of the budget
cut cut cut destroy the tanks for a cheap shot head a truck bomb the sleazy
little bit odd ball drop.*

*But they are the stallions of life.*

Cool long long haul. The battle continues. A lot more early he was a limb or a useful her dirty of a life in a new poll just to feel her. To you I mean engine. The feeling of the simplistic look even clicking clicking. But a lot of things that belong to the city today. She is looking to eat eat.

Listening to make these young looking all of the songs bloody well you know let me fucking Anglos will say yes or like the other infantile nothing. This is really very a little unsettling facility that he even the little ship that's been in the Lucy the tongue. Cities were open through the hands of such truthful men. To rule with the light of the laws should. On the earth.

You know as you did was say you were in that one of whom were jack off the other men no love with him been put into it but. Why do you get I mean yes I know that what I have taught you to be how long it is I'll be in. Luck I think to do to be how the he'll live to are they come one must be OK if you come let me come to morning. My mother to me. Will see blue can be seen to be bullies do something with loads of load on lock being loaded and I am running around the court with them over a clue.

Why don't you know going down the length of this is just not loving yourself to do no more even if you say I've not looked. I said you have your own head removed on her love but I do have a shot. I thought I was there no don't understand me or I'll have gotten better than the thought of the medicine man who thought I did not need to have to let me do it. Subtle little silk legs move to luck the muscle whom you call him relaxed their hearts filled with tranquillity. They strove for seeking sleep.

Look look look look look super super super skinny to get enough sleep. Looks to conclude the physics cyclicality into clicking it will be a little Kitty Kitty.

Never the burden of one man who would steer this vessel toward oblivion on the backs of the conquered. My course set by the eyeless visitors from above. Their mouths don't move and they speak inside my head. Never speak their name. The Lord has brought them unto you. The seed of the Father bears gifts and sorrows. They will call you home beyond the Sun before the paint is dry. As sure as you are born, they will call you home. As sure as you are born, they will live inside you. Nobility is not in action, it is in abstinence. Let them wilt inside us, their final home. Soon I will be forced to surrender in total and the reigns of

*this vessel will be handed over to the eyeless invaders. The country col-
lapses. The infrastructure collapses. Things are growing foggier. I don't
need the diagnosis. I know. I know as I always have and despaired. My
time grows ever shorter as the finish line grows ever closer.*

★★★

When I awoke I was alone in the house. Montblanc must
have started his day earlier than usual. I skipped breakfast and
instantly began writing about the man that I seemed to understand now better than ever before.

## 50

# PENOLOGIST

### Day 3

THOUGH HIS MIND had begun conditioning itself to resting atop flat concrete, his skull had yet to acclimate and the Convict awoke with a blue pain behind his eyes. He had dreamt about a raven-haired girl he remembered from his youth and his member now stood erect as a testament to her memory. The room was still paltry and square but seemed larger now than it had three days prior. The Convict made his way to the cell's sunken corner where he had been piling his stool and added to it with a malnourished and underwhelming offering. He had no idea what time it was and had no way of telling. From some reservoir of unspent hardiness, he set to completing the arbitrary number of press-ups he agreed upon during the night passed. His nose tapped the stone floor on each descent and his wiry arms revealed their thew, hinting at a dormant strength not yet fully dissolved, a strength that an untouchable life ago would be used to secure his current stone-walled tenure. The Convict sat heavy-shouldered on what was called his bed and stared at the unblinking walls. He thought about how much of the world he had seen and what he would never see again.

### Day 12

The pains of hunger had become affixed to the Convict's condition and were as regular to him now as breathing the staled air. He was delivered food exactly once per day, a solitary piece of cornbread so hard that it required water be poured over it before he could bite into it. The bread came at the same time each day, though whether this was meant to be breakfast or dinner he could not say. It was delivered by a gloved hand and dropped into the cell from a hole in the ceiling that remained covered at all other times. Each time the hole was uncovered the Convict tried to see who the gloved hand belonged to, but the process was over in a matter of seconds and the man up above never revealed his face. The exercise routine the Convict tried to maintain had begun to slip and he spent most of his time atop his stone bed thinking of ways he could pass the time but never finding strength enough to pursue any of them. He had grown visibly weaker and was sleeping longer each day. He dreamt of a vast field of yellow sunflowers, the brightness of which brought tears to his eyes.

### Day 38

The Convict had reduced to half the size he was at the time of his initial imprisonment. His face was sagged and gaunt and covered with patches of wiry hair. The hair on his head had thinned and more fell out each day. He collected the dead hair from around the cell and added it to a pile in the corner. With a little more hair and some clever craftsmanship, he figured he might be able to fashion something resembling a pillow. His arms and legs had shed their mass and muscularity revealing a network of protruding veins. His skin hung loose. His gums bled. The pile of stool in the sunken corner of the cell was slowly expanding, emanating a constant putrescence and further restricting the amount of habitable space. The convict's internal clock had adjusted to the daily delivery of cornbread and he could now correctly anticipate to the minute when the gloved hand would arrive to deliver him sustenance enough to live out another day. As he ate the cornbread, taking only the smallest of bites to prolong his enjoyment of it, the Convict concluded that the gloved hand keeping him alive must surely be that of God.

### Day 65

Though frail and sickly the Convict yet lived. His spine had started to curve and when he could find the resolve to stand he did so at a height now markedly lessened. He felt cold. He felt little else. On this sixty-fifth day of imprisonment, the hole in the roof was uncovered and the Convict's mouth began to salivate in anticipation, but no gloved hand emerged and no bread was dropped, rather a voice called to the Convict. The first voice he had heard since his quarantine began.

"Is it your desire to be free?"

The Convict did not respond. He negotiated the scenario with what little wits he still maintained. He had lost the memory of many things and though he was teased with the images of a past life in his dreams he knew in this exact moment that he was not asleep and that he was not dead. The voice called again.

"Is it your desire to be free?"

The Convict had accepted early on that freedom remained starkly outside the realm of possibility. He had stayed alive simply by impulse and not by mismanaged fancies of freedom or release. And yet, here he hears the herald's query. He had not tried speaking for many days and he found it difficult to get his words out now. With what strength remained he tried in desperation to answer the voice from up high, though what came out was but a hoarse and weakened croak.

"I will ask it of you once again, but please, hurry. Is it your desire to be free?"

The Convict's voice continues to fail him as he struggles to be heard by the stranger in the sky. He can offer nothing but a dusty wheeze.

"I fear I must leave before they return. This is your last chance, friend. Do you desire to be freed?"

His body fights him throughout every motion, but the Convict manages to stand up and slightly reduce the distance between himself and the open hole to freedom. He cups his hands around his mouth, his long and yellowed fingernails tangling amidst one another, and shouts with whatever strength still lingered within him. But all that came out was a coarse whisper unheard by the mysterious man above.

"And so it is. I cannot force your freedom upon you. Goodbye, friend."

The hole in the roof closes and the Convict sinks back to his stone bed where he lies curled like an embryo. He falls asleep and dreams of rusted hacksaws wielded by angels of light.

## 51

## POTATIONS

"DRINK WITH ME."

These were the words M sternly spoke as he walked through the door of the office where I had been working feverishly and efficiently all day. These were also the first words that he had spoken to me since he caught me trespassing in his bedroom last night—the fallout of which was still unknown to me. It was just after five and though this was only an hour shy of my usual stopping time I was, perhaps out of the guilt and embarrassment I felt for last night's actions, enjoying a rare surge of productivity that I was not particularly inclined to cut short. But then, 'drink with me', spoken with an edge sharp enough to slice through my fettered focus. This giant boulder blowing through the door, intent on breaking the fast of Ramadan and scattering the shoals collected in the shallow waters of my throat. Halfway to Ascension and now the captain orders us to throw anchor?

I saw in his right hand a bottle of brown booze adorned with a label I didn't recognize, and in his left two identical glasses small enough to fit in his palm. I see where he wants this to go and I suspect that he's picked up on my apprehension.

"The book can wait, this cannot. Drink with me."

Now while I'm tempted to tell Max that at this moment I would rather write about him than talk to him, I know better than to bite the ample hand of the benefactor. I save my work mid-sentence and close the document, hoping that I'll remember how to finish the thought when I open it again tomorrow. Interpreting this action as acceptance of his offer, Monty takes a seat across the table from me. He's still wearing his 'work' clothes—whatever that means. Was he in Toronto or Ottawa today? Who cares. I'm thirty years old and I don't know how to tie a tie. I don't even own a tie and I've deluded myself into affirming that as some point of pride. I don't know what a Double Windsor is, but you can shove it up your ass for all I care. Okay, apparently there's some lingering aggression I had better shake off. Great big smiles now, fake it 'til you make it and all that.

As M sits down I try to read the label on the bottle. It's 'Mac' something or other. Mac means Scottish right? Scottish means whisky? Or is it rye? Is there a difference? In my limited experience it always results in the same disgusting shudder as it slides down my throat. Occasionally Maxime and I would have wine on the nights we had dinner together. Even then I have to work hard to feign polite gesticulations as I force the rotten grapes into my body. What can I say? I'm a simple man when it comes to these things. My drink of choice is beer that I see in commercials. I don't own a tie.

Regardless, Max and I have never indulged in anything like this, but I suppose it is in my best interest to humour him. No brakes on this gravy train. No screaming women tied to the railroad tracks. Still wordless, he goes about filling both of our glasses with the mystery elixir. I feel a little tight in the chest, like the nervous anticipation you get before the drugs kick in—or so I'm told. When he's done pouring, he lifts his glass in the air, holding it toward me. I mirror his gesture like a properly socialized person would—or so I'm told.

"All at once now. *Santé.*"

### The First Drink

AHG! POISON! Goddamn is that ever vile! It's burning my throat. Why hasn't it stopped yet? Christ, am I going to die? This is how I go out? Hunched over a table a million miles from home, choking on Mac-what's-his-name's Scottish venom? Oh, wait, the pain is going away. Okay, I can breathe again. I feel it boiling in my belly, but despite my near-death experience, I manage to maintain composure on the outside. I think. Monty didn't seem to notice either way as he now starts to lighten the load that has so clearly been encumbering his mind since he walked in.

"Thank you for joining me, Lawrence. While indeed there is no shortage of political colleagues with which I may have shared this drink, one in my position must be cautious, as each drink with them is never just a simple drink. Each drink with them is a statement. An affirmation of alliance or allegiance, an opportunity to forge the links that bind us. It becomes tiresome when all you truly desire is company and companionship."

He pauses a moment.

"It can be very dangerous to make friends in this business."

Call it motherly intuition, but I sense that little Maxy may have had a rough day. He has generally been adamant about not sharing any details of his day-to-day affairs with me, encouraging me instead to concern myself with his past, but I wonder if right now he's willing to make an exception. He doesn't seem to be angry with me, but there's something that he wants to talk about. Why else are we doing this? I'll press him a bit.

"How do you, how do you mmmm-muh-mmmm-mean?"

"Nothing in need of decryption, my friend. I speak plain truth as two sharing a drink should. It can be very dangerous to make friends in my business. Friendship clouds your better judgement. It gives way to attachments and sentimentalities that can hide the obvious decisions that need to be made. We had to make, *I* had to make a choice today that betrayed the trust of someone who I sincerely enjoy. He is what you or I or anyone else would consider to be a good man. Honest, loyal, altruistic even if you believe in such a thing. Today an immovable wall was placed in front of his career, a wall constructed on my order. By all accounts it was the right decision. While I respected his integrity and honour, such traits can be liabilities in this world. From here on he will occupy only a trivial role in my campaign, and while I have long since accepted the distinction between what is right and what is required, I find myself uneasy with this decision. His face when I told him was akin to a dog that had been abused by its master. There can be no friends at the poker table if you expect to come out on top."

As he finishes his thought, the moonlighting bartender proceeded to fill our glasses once again. I should have known that I wasn't going to get out of here that easily. From this point our conversations become spotted and fecund, they trail off and bleed into one another, our words winding like streams as my tongue slowly comes to terms with the Scottish solution that every quarter hour was reintroduced. Bear with me as I tune this radio.

### The Second Drink

"How is it that you are able to be here, Lawrence? You hastily accepted my offer of employment knowing full well it would take several months. Have you no attachments back home? Is there no one eagerly awaiting your return?"

And I don't remember how it happened, but I soon found myself going through the details of my last romantic relationship with M, something I hadn't ever done with anyone else. Maybe I felt secure discussing this with someone who was so far removed, or maybe it was just the hooch unscrewing my inhibitions, but I told him everything. I told him that when I asked her what she was passionate about in life she responded by saying that she was passionate about me. I told him how disgusted that made me feel, how I didn't want to take on that responsibility. I told him how her devotion threatened my way of life. I told him how I wasn't able to end it with any shred of integrity, opting instead to let things linger and disintegrate until I could convince her that I was nothing more than a burden. He listened to me. He listened to me intently, and for the first time in recent memory I felt like my jagged words were being processed, and not just tolerated.

"I empathize, and truly I do. I would not embarrass us both by attempting to speak about matters of love in any certainties, but I do know that you retain opportunities that I do not and I would urge you not to squander them. Be civil with your desires, but do not follow my lead on this. What is dead for me may yet find life within you."

### The Third Drink

It's worth mentioning that alcohol is one of the precious few things that seems to help with my stuttering. After a few drinks most words tend to come a lot easier to me. I've read that it has something to do with the alcohol 'relaxing' the brain and curbing some of the anxieties that might cause the stutter. And now you're thinking, 'so why don't you just drink more then?' Gee, great question. Maybe I should start each morning with three fingers of my preferred brand. I don't see any harm in that whatsoever.

"Do you know what it is that we're drinking?"

"Can't say I d–d–do."

"It's a Scotch. Macmillan. About three thousand a bottle as I recall."

And suddenly I hear police sirens coming for me as if I've stolen from the school treasury or the church collection plate. I'll crunch the numbers later but I'm pretty sure we've just drank what would be roughly the equivalence of one month's rent back home in less than an hour.

"Three g-grand? Muh–Max you shouldn't have."

"Please, have you any idea how many 'three grands' I have? And who else would I drink this with? How do you find it?"

"The truth?"

"The truth."

"It's wuh–wasted on me. It all tastes the, tastes the same."

"Do you recall Aesop's Fable about the Miser and his gold?"

"No, I grew up with TV."

"Clever boy. As it goes, there was once an old Miser who spent his life collecting gold and burying it at the foot of a tree beside his house. Every so often he would dig up his gold collection, admire his prizes, and rebury them. One day a Robber noticed this behaviour, and when the Miser was asleep, the Robber dug up the gold and stole it for himself. The next day the Miser discovered that all of his gold has gone missing and he fell to his knees, screaming in agony. When his neighbours came to comfort him, they suggested that he place some rocks in the hole where the gold used to be. After all, he only ever looked upon the gold, surely he could do the same thing with the rocks. Now drink up."

### The Fourth Drink

"What will you do after this?"

"Go to b-b-bed probably."

"Once the book is finished, Larry. What will you do once the book is finished? You'll have money. Money opens doors. What do you intend to pursue?"

"Try to ruh-write maybe."

"That pleases me to hear, though I prophesy a myriad of troubles for you. If I may offer one piece of advice—do not write with them in mind. Linger on the nature of art if you will. Is appearance always the point? Is it true to create something without the audience in mind? I'd not wish these burdens on you. I'd rather your efforts be buried under the sands of history than diluted by your expectations of expectations.

### The Fifth Drink

"No, no, it's *santé*, not 'san-tay.' *Santé*. Hear the difference? This is important. Try again.

"C-caah-can't you just t-teach me, teach me some swear words instead?"

"We'll get there. But first I promise that we will refine you if it takes us all night."

### The Sixth Drink

"Then you should know better than to wear the themes of your ordeals like a self-adhesive name tag. I cannot speak with more clarity than I offer you now. Ours is a story of two men similar in many ways, one powerful, the other forgotten. This brings me no joy, but the juxtaposition is not one I can ignore— and surely you have thought of it as well. We both came from nothing. We both see the world in a similar way. Both our paths have lead us here and we are now both sitting as the same table, drinking from the same bottle. So where did our trajectories so radically diverge as to lead me to the bowels of Ottawa while you fester away in under-achieving obsoletion? I know where you place your blames, but do you truly believe that were you born a foot taller and with no blades in your throat that you would soar to the heights you see behind your eyes? There are no bigger barriers in life than the ones that we ourselves erect."

And while M's words should have offended me, or stirred me, or inspired me, what they really did was exonerate me. I may be a hack and an underachiever, but I've never been caught misquoting Ronald Reagan.

### The Seventh Drink

And here things get muddled. I can't remember the drinks that followed or the intricacies of the conversations surrounding them. The last thing I can remember with any clarity or certainty were the words that Montblanc spoke shortly after imbibing our seventh. It was something along the lines of:

"You are not my friend, Lawrence. I do not have any right to make that claim. It seems the higher I rise the fewer friends I am allowed to retain. And soon our time together will end. The job will be done and we will likely never see each other again. You will go about your life and make of it what you will while I do the same. That is not friendship. Still, I would be doing us both a dishonour if I did not acknowledge my appreciation of you at this very moment. For whatever it is worth to you, I am truly grateful for the present company. *Je te remercie.* Oh, and one last thing."

"What's that?"

"I still have several bottles of this Scotch remaining in my stores. Disobey my rules again and I promise you that we will drink every last one of them."

## 52

# PISCATOLOGY

THERE ARE OCCASIONAL days when one must accept that nothing productive is going to get done. The earlier one can acknowledge this the more hours may be spared from contrition. Here we are on such a day, floating serenely atop the warm waters of acceptance. No hauling of scattered history, no polishing of past relics, just a nothing day to be stricken from the official records. Motivation is limited and inspiration cannot be forced, even when the carrot on the end of the stick is worth about five years. A true nothing day indeed. I'll assure you now that you'll find nothing here to advance the plot. I tell you this as a courtesy—that you might skip ahead freely and without guilt should you desire more immediate narrative placation.

Okay then.

I awoke late in the morning with a suffocated brain and a mouth still soured from the, uh, 'merriment' of the prior evening. Somehow Montblanc had already managed to get up and leave the house for whatever great adventure he was meant to have, but as for me, well, after embracing the fruitlessness and futility of the day I decided to spend what remained of it from the comfort of Montblanc's picturesque backyard. Direct sunlight, I call upon you to replenish my vitamin D supply and to char my chalky casing. A serendipitous combination of fortunes adding to the resplendence of the scenery. First, the unblocked sun, next, the isolation. M shouldn't be home until the evening, while the groundskeeper is apparently not on duty today.

A brief note on the groundskeeper—I myself have never spoken to him, and have seen only flashes of his form through the window of the guestroom. I was alerted the first time this happened and it took more than a moment to realize who the stranger in Maxime's yard was and what he was doing there, the concept of paid grounds work alien to me. The groundskeeper, M refers to him as 'Mack', though one could safely assume this was not his given name, is a tanned Asian man of seemingly infinite stamina. Some mornings I can hear snippets of his conversations with Monty, who he refers to with his strong accent exclusively and at the end of every sentence as 'boss.' He starts work early, long before I'm out of bed, and he has unknowingly taken on the role of my unofficial alarm clock, waking me up with his puttering and mowing and green-thumbing by the window. I feel guilty every time this happens. Mack is up and labouring away while I'm unhurried under expensive sheets. This is why I'm glad that he's not here today. The tranquility of my current situation would surely be compromised if Mack was pruning and deadheading around my indolent body. Montblanc's backyard is gorgeous in a way that is beyond my ability to describe, and this is due largely to Mack's regularly applied expertise. But when it comes time to enjoy the fruits of his labour, I can't have him anywhere near the scene. That right there is why I could never be rich enough to have my own personal staff. I recoil at the thought of anyone working for me. My shoes could never be shined by any hands but mine. Yes, I belong on my hands and knees toiling beside Mack and exchanging harmless subversions, not lying on the grass he has so perfectly maintained as I am now. In any case, I felt it necessary to commit a paragraph toward appropriately lauding Mack, my comrade of Montblanc's employ, a man who works hard and never complains. Here's to you brother. And now back to me.

The grass where I'm lying, a nutritious bed of deep green, has a subtle hint of moisture and each individual blade feels like a velvet tendril on my bare back. My eyes closed, my hands behind my head, I feel small insects using my stomach as a landing strip, a brief layover in their indeterminate journeys. A stream runs through the backyard into nearby Lake Ontario offering a persistent auditory relaxant. I'll purposefully avoid attempting to further describe the scene in significant detail. I think that's better left to you. Regardless, in this exact moment it's hard to feel anything beyond peace.

But what peace ever endures?

My own was compromised when I started to hear the noises. A low rumble, a murmuring sound, barely discernable at first but slowly escalating in volume and urgency. I kept still for a moment, focusing on the strange noise and attempting to identify its origin point. Interjected with the murmuring were sporadic high-pitched pangs and wails, and though audible, these sounds were muffled as if they were coming from underground. The hands of anxiety fumble around with my innards. These were not the pacifying sounds of nature that had moments ago lulled me into equanimity—these were the sounds of agony emitted by a host that was clearly suffering. I sit up and feel my back dampen with sweat. The sunlight had transitioned from welcome caretaker to a liability as I felt the direct heat further disorient my senses. The high-pitch wails, resembling a cross between a bird's chirp and the whine of an abused dog, were starting to increase in frequency. Scanning the environs, my head darting back and forth like a startled rooster, I notice nothing unordinary.

And then, a splash from the stream.

I stand up and uneasily make my way to the water. As I look down my heart expands and threatens to tear a hole through my chest. In the stream, itself only about three feet wide, I see, stuck amid the rocks and shallow water, the struggling body of *Acipenser transmontanus*—the white sturgeon. The largest species of freshwater fish that can be found in all of North America. But I knew right away that this wasn't a regular white sturgeon. This was Praegrandis and he was near-death.

A brief note on Praegrandis—but first, a rudimentary understanding of white sturgeon is required. Only then will you be able to properly emphasize with the terror currently coursing through me.

<u>WHITE STURGEON</u>       A REPORT BY LARRY MANN

*White sturgeon, like all species of sturgeon, are among some of the oldest underwater creatures ever discovered, believed to have first appeared over 200 million years ago. They have evolved remarkably little since and are considered to be living fossils. White sturgeon are big (generally around six to eight feet in length), and they live a long time (some even see their centennial). They are found exclusively in the river systems of Western North America, most prominently in British Columbia, Washington, and California. They are bottom feeders who use their suction-like mouths to scoop food from riverbeds. They do not pose a threat to humans, and are sometimes fished for sport, though usually released as their meat can potentially be toxic.*

As for Praegrandis, I remember first hearing whispers of him when I was about eight years old on a camping trip with my family just outside of Lillooet (that's on the Fraser River, where Praegrandis allegedly dwells). 150 years old they say, and twenty feet long—a true monster. I remember my dad, red ball cap on and with a can of beer in his hand saying with no hint of jest, 'don't go in the river or he'll swallow you whole.' His playfully disguised warning against swimming in the swift and potentially dangerous waters of the river planted a seed in my psyche that later blossomed into a fully realized phobia that is still hung within me. Today, I fully enjoy the sight, sounds, and smells of running water, as I had been this afternoon, yet I must admit that I am still afraid to submerge any part of my body within those moving waters. Praegrandis would always be waiting, ready to pull me under and devour me whole. An irrational fear, yes, but accepting that doesn't alleviate it any.

And now back to the matter at hand.

After twenty-some years of successful avoidance, I am now standing above Praegrandis, the mighty white sturgeon more than three times my length. Still frozen in fear, I don't bother to address how a creature native to Western Canada has found itself in a stream in Southern Ontario. That's not important right now. Right now I've a trial ahead of me and I've not yet decided how to proceed. Praegrandis is thrashing and weeping, his colossal body wedged in the shallow water and rocks of a stream that is narrower than he is. Left alone he will die here. I can watch the entirety of this fate. I can witness my fears being erased as the omnipresent monster is finally removed from the veins of water I've been too afraid to feel. I will finally be able to baptize myself and be born anew from safe waters. I will finally be able to float for endless days in serenity and bliss.

But in this moment I can already feel the hollowness such a victory would bring.

I am looking at Praegrandis. I haven't stopped looking since my eyes initially found him. This is not the agent of my nightmares that I've conditioned myself to fear—this is a creature that needs my help, a creature that will die without my intervention. Am I to become my own warden? Am I to lock myself tighter into the binds of horror by releasing the very demon I've made a lifelong attempt at escaping? My mettle is bending under the weight of this choice and I fear it's about to snap entirely. What could I even do? Lift him free? He weighs as much as a buffalo. And even if I managed to free him, what's to stop him from getting trapped again? Will I have to touch it? What if he really does swallow me? If only Mack were here, he would know what to do. His crying is getting louder still. I feel his wails ricochet inside my skull as my guilt mounts. What am I meant to do?

Goddammit fish, you're over a century old, shouldn't you have learned how to avoid getting stuck by now? This stream isn't wide enough for you. What were you thinking? Why are you here in the first place? Where are you even going? These waters were calm before you showed up. Now you're splashing all over the place, making me feel guilt that you haven't earned. I don't know how to save you. I don't even know if I want to. Jesus Christ! I didn't ask to be put in this position! I was fine avoiding you. We had a good thing going on. I hate you but I don't want to watch you die like this, it's not what you deserve. But maybe you don't have to go out alone. Maybe that's what I can offer you. Oh great Praegrandis, I will be joining you in your journey to the other side. If you're stuck, then I will be too.

And then? My decision making skills were still blitzed by the torrent of stimuli I was exposed to. The sun melting my brain. The screams of this ancient creature assaulting my eardrums. My fears and phobias sewn on my sleeves. My honour under cross-examination. And then? I jumped into the stream, submitting myself to whatever happened next.

And then my eyes opened and I found myself still lying on the perfectly maintained grass. There was no noise beyond the running water and the singing birds. There was no dying beast in the stream. Of course there wasn't. Why would there be? In my placidity I had fallen asleep and the sun must have perverted my thoughts, causing me to dream of myself in an absurd situation. I felt overheated and still had a bit of a headache. The blades of grass that earlier felt of velvet now felt sharp and itchy on my back.

There are occasional days when one must accept that nothing productive is going to get done. I call them nothing days. Today was meant to be one of those days. I think it still might be. Regardless, I think that's enough sunshine for one day. Time to go in.

But first I find in myself the resolve to wash my face with the revitalizing waters of the gently moving stream.

# 53

## PANOPTICISM

WITH LATE NIGHTS come fleeting moments of acute lucidity. My head is shuffled like the feet of pagans and everything I know about myself is pending confirmation. The impeccably tailored are standing at attention as the tarnished influence of Oedipus is hurled against the interior walls. I feel a guest in my own guise, a jester justifiably juxtaposed beside the trueborn heroes who would never just stop at just enough. The cherubs working the theatre tonight have been considerate enough to wake me for the intermission so that I might realign my sight toward the vacant stage. Red drapery conceals the walls and golden handrails guide the guests toward their seats. I never stop conjecting about what happens on the other side of the stage curtain. Just as I can find some reassurance in the present moment the windows close and the next act begins.

And such visions with their totalizing embrace!

I take the stage first as a comedian, and while the audience erupts as I enter, I notice each of them are wearing the same floral-pattern shirt as I am. As my act is expected to begin I realize that I have no material prepared. I point out that tonight's crowd has a keen fashion sense. They laugh. I stall as I try to remember any decent jokes. They stop laughing. The room grows quiet. I ask them how they are doing tonight. I see people standing up to leave. Finally, I recall that joke about the elephant and the shoemaker, but it was already too late.

I take the stage a second time, this time as the band's lead guitarist. Elation so loud as we take our positions that I can't hear the drummer count us in. The song begins and I still don't know how to play the guitar.

It's the night of my ten-year high school reunion. I've decided to go and then not go about a dozen times. I think about what
to expect. I think about *Restoring Conviction,* the British Columbia
bestseller that I wouldn't be able to talk about. I wouldn't be able
to talk about anything. I'm host to a moment of lamentation as I
accept that I will not be able to tell Sophia Watt that I used to
write her poems that I still have in a box under my bed.

I'm back home in my hovel on Saint Helena Island, sleeping
soundly in the proximity of Napoleon's original grave. I've come
to this, one of the most remote locations on the planet, to work
in isolation on the novel that will define my career. The coffee is
incredible and the locals are respectful of my space.

I'm on my deathbed. The doctor must have noticed my lack
of visitors as he is spending a disproportionate amount of time with
me. He stays with me even after his shift has ended. My social link
with him is the last I will form before dying in obscurity.

The metallurgists are working with the alloys provided. I
trust them as I trust the pharmacist. I know that when I wake
from these visions the efforts of their labour will carry me
through another day. If I lead a march, I'd still get lost along the
way. If I wrote a speech, I'd still forget what to say. They once
gave me a small cube of pure silver to suck on. 'Can you taste the
difference?' But taste the difference I could not! My palate is not
so refined as to ignore the sour and acidic notes assaulting my
mouth each night. I explained this to Dr. Freud with candor and
sincerity as he nodded his head and chomped on his cigar. You
provoke me good doctor! Can you explain how the human body
is able to contort in such ways and why such contortions are not
replicable under honest light?

I've been practicing silent meditation recently. What's your
professional opinion on this? See, I read a book written by this
Eastern fellow, and he said that in times of sadness or anxiety that
I should recite a small mantra to myself. 'Smile in the present
moment, for it is a beautiful moment.' And so, I tried smiling and
repeating those words to myself in times of trouble. The irony of
course is that I only repeated these words in times of anxiety and
now I've been conditioned to feel anxious whenever I think of

them. I don't want you to consult with Dr. Pavlov, I only want to keep my focus unbroken when the Gestapo start pounding on my door.

These moving pictures are provided without the context and baggage of inciting incidents, sufficient conflict, or believable characters. Strain your neck upwards and you will see, standing high above any of the aforementioned fears, piercing the clouds and tickling the heavens, the archon of futility whose stoic hand guides both the waking and dormant doubt I dwell on. I've been doing this wrong my entire life, but still, I've been doing it my entire life. My aim is not to satiate your need for resolution—I happily leave that to hands more capable than my own. But if there is a brazier within you that cannot be lit by conventional arrangements, then may I be so bold as to request the formation of our perfect union. I need you. If you only knew how badly I need you. I'm losing balance. I presented the keyholder with a feast of rare and foreign ingredients and he ate only the bread. He told me to throw everything else out. Don't you get it? There would be nothing left. The collection plate would remain perennially empty. I am speaking directly to you now. Hidden on this page and in this paragraph the remnants of my scattered plea take form. Don't let them take me away. Without you there will be nothing to stop them. I know you see things as I do. You wouldn't be here elsewise. To avoid suspicion I will now make a subtle transition back to a cohesive narrative that should serve to placate the circling vultures overhead.

★★★

I awake with sweaty palms and a strange erection to the sound of a loud crash upstairs. Sweaty because I had been overwhelmed by advancing enemy forces and strange because I had not previously learned how to connect lust with escape attempts. There's something about the air in Oshawa that causes the cilia in my lungs to work double quick.

Still in my sleepwear I head upstairs and find the source of the crash—Montblanc had collapsed at the base of the steps leading to his bedroom. He wasn't getting up.

## 54

## PENETRALIA

I OFFER M a hand up that he doesn't accept, opting instead to pull himself up proper with the help of the nearby bannister. I ask him if he's okay. He says he's fine and thank you. I tell him that I'll get him a glass of water. I do. He's sitting on the chesterfield in the living room when I return from the kitchen. I place the water on the coffee table in front of him and take the empty seat on the other side of it. He thanks me again. He assures me that he's fine and that I should go back to bed now. He says it's late and there's much to do tomorrow and I should just go back to bed.

And I want to do exactly that. But I don't.

I look into his eyes. It's around midnight and I can hear a light rain tapping the ground outside. I'm still looking at him. I'm wearing a sleeveless undershirt and I feel my arms beginning to shake—a little cold, mostly nervous. I'm still looking at him. I can't give a single inch. Anticipation and defiance and a silent war. He knows what's happening. He's never lost a battle in his life. His eyes sharpen but mine remain unmoved. I was not born to fight. He leans in slightly. He rests his elbows atop his knees and his chin atop his hands. And he speaks. Each word over-enunciated and too loud for the silent room.

"To bed now, Lawrence."

Adhering to this demand would be the smart thing to do. But I don't. I hold my ground. My arms are still shaking. I run the words through my head over and over again paying close attention to every syllable. I take a deep breath and relax my diaphragm.

"What's wruh-wrong with you?"

"It's late and you are tired, and as such I can overlook your boldness. I regret that you found me in such a state, but there is much to be done tomorrow so at this point I must insist that you return down those stairs and back to bed."

I've taken steps to avoid confrontation my entire life but I'm at the breach now and I've come too far to turn around. I'm staring at the gift horse's mouth. I'm biting the feeding hand. I'm thinking only in idioms.

"Max, what's wrrrrong with you?"

"Enough now! Do not speak to me familiar as if you were a friend! You are here to do a specific job and that alone. Do you think yourself the only person with any shred of literary puissance? Do you not know the rapidity with which you could be replaced? This conversation is over. You best leave right now and thank the grace of God that I am willing to forget it ever happened. Press the issue any further and I swear to the highest heaven that by tomorrow you'll find yourself on a plane headed back to the insignificant corner of the world whence you came."

His right arm has started moving at the elbow as if he were turning an invisible crank. I've noticed him make those type of movements before but I never thought much of it. While I continue to look at him I think about my apartment back home and the mattress in the corner of my room. I think about how adept I've become at living frugally the discipline I've developed to spend my limited income only on things I really need. I think about all the ways in which M's paycheque could change my life. But then none of that seemed to matter.

"Max. Wuh–what's wrong with you?"

And as I brace myself for his response snippets of memories begin to form as a cohesive collage. I remember the scattered words I saw written in the book at the bottom of his bedside table. I remember what he told me about 'the blackness inside his father.' I remember all his talk of parasites and of legacy. I remember that he has made a conscious decision to father no children. I remember all his strange behaviours that I had previously attributed to his eccentric personality. And suddenly I am a drowning man finally coming up for air. In that moment he was no longer Maxime Montblanc the Magnificent sitting across from me. He wasn't the unstoppable business magnate nor was he the undefeatable parliamentarian. He wasn't the future Prime Minister and he wasn't the pinnacle of perfection I had grown accustom to. He was a man. He was a man, and he wasn't well.

He stood up, but before he could deliver the fervorous and thunderous verbal assault I knew was coming I let slip my question on instinct and with all the fumbling tact of a curious child.

"You're s-s-suh-sick, aren't you?"

And there stood speechless the man of infinite words. Maybe it was hearing those words spoken out loud by someone else, but his demeanor had radically shifted from one of aggression to one of vulnerability. In brazen silence he sat back down across from me. He runs his hands through his hair and exhales, his shoulders shrinking as he does.

"Let no one ever doubt the shrewdness of your mind, but your company in any of this was never my intention. Do you truly wish to pursue these credentials, as bare as I warn you they are?"

I tell him that I do and he nods slightly and slowly. He turns his head toward the window and stares at the trees in his backyard partially veiled now by a thin curtain of rain. Seconds crawl tensely by and I know that he won't start speaking until he knows exactly what to say. That it's taken him this long to collect his words suggests that this is something he hasn't often spoken about.

"I feel myself breathing as I never once needed to. I feel the limitations of my body knelt and sore. I feel the burdens of age and in this I am not unique. Yet I do not feel everything. My flesh and mind betray my intentions and act increasingly of their own volition, satisfying the agenda of some devilish invader. Even in death my father's shadow remains cast large, enveloping all of me. He would drag me into the Earth alongside him. There's a sun setting within me and it is not one that shall ever rise again. Everything I hope to accomplish is a race against this fading light and challenged by a mind and body that grow more unreliable by the day. And how intensely have I raged against this fate. My onset delayed, my condition hidden, my momentum maintained, all through sheer force of will. But still, there is no ceasing what comes for me."

"Wuhh-what comes for you?"

"That which comes for all of us in due time. There is no tragedy in this. Rather, mine is defined by my unwillingness to gamble with the Devil's deck, even when promised dead equal odds."

"Muh-Mmmmax, puh-please, t-t-t-tuh-tuh-tuh-tuh-talk normal."

"Talk normal . . . Is this advice you offer me, Larry? Is it a mirroring of what you have wished for yourself your entire life? I know you will not believe it but your bravery continues to astound me. Very well then. You fight boldly through the frustration and chagrin of your eviscerated words and I should be rightly expected to do the same. The truth of it then."

Max stops speaking to watch the rain. While I wait for him to arrange his words I think once again about my apartment back home and my empty mattress in the corner of my bedroom. There once was a proper bedframe but it broke and I've never bothered to replace it. Some time before it broke I sat on that bed with her, she who might still be sitting on it today under different circumstances. The last time we sat together on that bed I was looking out the window, just as Max is now, thinking on all the things I might say. She wanted to hear anything, but I gave her nothing. I resented her expectation. After she had gone and it became clear that she wouldn't ever have reason to come back, I wrote about the encounter with borrowed words. I wonder how many years I have left before the memory of her face disappears entirely.

"The doctors called it Huntington's disease, but in truth I knew my father's mind was bent from the beginning. His descent was not one of lesions or holes that might be so easily bandaged and covered. Before the shaking and the wheelchair and the official diagnosis there was the changing of his words. He began to speak of incidents that never occurred and of family members that never existed. He was always an inwardly pious man, if he ever felt the touch of God this was not something he would have ever cared to share. That too changed. He claimed eschatological visions and soon began screaming late at night about fallen angels and the end of days. And soon it was that my father, a simple man who placed great value on the importance of hard work and other such traditional notions, became unwilling to leave his bed. Some time later my mother forced him to the sages in white who would diagnose him. I left home shortly after to begin my career but before I could make my first million he was dead. But not before bestowing upon me his parting gift."

"Puh-puh-puh-parrrrting g-g-gift?"

"This condition that claimed my father's body and mind is of course a potentially hereditary one."

Enola Gay, you have permission to deliver your payload.

"Have you, have you, have you, have you been t-tuh-tuh-tested?"

"No, and nor do I need to be. I can already feel it inside me. As sure as it killed my father so too will it soon come for me. But not before . . ."

He stops midsentence, something I don't recall ever happening. I can never seem to get out of my own head, though right now I can't seem to get in it. I pray time might pass unmolested.

"But not before I have managed to leave something behind."

He finishes the fractured sentence and my eyes light up and then sink under this new burden of sincerity.

"And surely in your insight you have now come to the truth of it."

"Your wuh-wuh-wuh-wuh-wife—"

"Is halfway across the country trying in desperation to become pregnant with another man. She is fast becoming dry and this may well be her last chance to carry the child that I once promised her."

Max leans back, folds his arms, and tilts his head upward to look at the roof.

"In my father I saw weakness and mediocrity and as a young man I was determined to surpass him in every way. And by all measures surpass him I have. I also believed that all my success in life would be for naught if I hadn't any children with which to share it. Above all else I knew I could have been a better father than he was. But which is the greater sin? Denying myself the children I intended to care for with the entirety of my capacities, or passing on to them the same defective genes that might also lay premature claim to their lives? And so was the gamble I never chanced. And in my guilt and in my denial I reasoned that despite not leaving a familial legacy behind I may yet leave a legacy of comparable importance. The legacy of a Prime Minister. And with that I might burn my name into the pages of history before succumbing to my father's debt."

"Muh-muh-m-m-m-m-muh-muh-Max I d-d-d-d-duh-don't—"

"Pay it no further mind, dear Lawrence. Though it hangs precarious above me as the rusted Sword of Damocles my end is not upon me yet. And neither is yours. You have a condition and it is one that you rightfully curse, but you have a life ahead of you that will be full and wide. I myself find a comfort in that, I should think that you may as well. But I am afraid that you simply must excuse me. My mind is wearied and must be returned to a condition that the tasks of tomorrow necessitate. Such is the mechanism of all things."

And without wasting a second to linger on what was just said Max places his hands on his knees and hoists his large frame up from the chesterfield with an audible groan that plays repeatedly in my head. He reaches the staircase but before ascending he turns his attention to me once more.

"Oh, and Lawrence?"

I turn my head and raise my chin toward him.

"Apologies for raising my voice. *Mes manières m'échappent au pire des temps.*"

And then he disappeared up the staircase leaving me alone in the room that was dark save for midnight's muted light. I didn't get up right away. I didn't get up for quite some time. I sat there on Montblanc's pristine furniture in a way that few others likely have. And as I sat there I finally realized something that should have been clear to me for a long time now.

I am not happy with the state of my life.

## 55

# PATHOGENESIS

EVERYTHING IS BREAKING and everything is falling apart and aging and dusty and decrepit and decaying and derelict and dilapidated and disintegrating. Nothing is working properly and it's all falling apart. I think about how much dust my apartment must have gathered. It was dusty when I left. And it's all broken. There's a chipped mug on my desk and it's full of pens that don't have any ink. My microwave has been broken for six months and I haven't bothered to move or replace it. It's all breaking down. The white rubber tips on the toes of my Chucks, once a luminous white, are now stained with dead grass and dirt. Fading and aging and the plumbing doesn't work right. It drips all night and I can hear it in my dreams. I'm breaking. I'm getting fatter and slower and I can't get up in the mornings. The screw on my glasses is loose and now the frames wiggle. The enamel on my teeth has worn down and now they hurt when I eat anything with sugar in it. It's fading and breaking and nothing is working. My white shirts are all stained at the pits. My bookshelf is covered in dust and moths are eating my sweaters. And there's dust and I breathe it in and it settles in my lungs. And there's mass graves in the jungles and in the frontiers and their dirt is cold and can't be washed off. Everything fades and people don't remember my face. There's a metallic taste in my mouth and I don't know if it's coming from malfunctioning organs within or from the rusty air outside. Old papers with poems are stained yellow. My computer is contaminated with viruses and spyware and malware and nothing is working anymore. The mouse and the keyboard are covered in dust and grime and dead skin and oil. The wheels on my suitcase have fallen off and I'm not strong enough to carry it for very long. There's visible particles dancing around in my glass of tap water and I drink it anyway because my better judgement is broken. The carpet is ugly and crusted with vegetable juice and the walls are smoke-stained. Everything is breaking and decayed and nothing is working the way it was meant to. There are creases all over the covers of Joyce and Cohen and their innards smell of smoke and earth. The cuffs of my sweaters and shirts are tattered and frayed and stretched and nothing fits quite right anymore. Nothing works right and everything is dusty. A diversity of dead insects is collected in the lampshade, buried under a blanket of dust. I dig my grave with a spade that has a broken handle. There's a pain in my lower back when I sit in the same place for too long because I'm decaying and breaking and I'm forgetting the sounds of the voices I once knew. The skin on my feet is cracked and dried. I want to ask my maker for input but I've forgotten how to take the prayer position. My wits are fading and my vocabulary is fading and everything else is breaking. There's plastic duct-taped to the window where the glass broke over a year ago.

Everything is breaking and everything is falling apart, yes, but I am still here. I am still here and I have the privilege of being able to selectively ignore the surrounding decay when I need to. But Montblanc? Well he's breaking in a way that can't be fixed, isn't he?

## 56

# PROGNOSTICATION

I HAD NOTICED certain oddities in M's physical mannerisms before. A subtle shaking of his shoulders, an occasional jerk in his walk, though prior to last night's confession I never thought much of it. It's not as if he ever seemed troubled or needed help of any kind. As for his numerous personality idiosyncrasies, well those I just chalked up to the eccentricities that are to be expected from the rich, powerful, and charismatic. But I retain now the Forbidden Knowledge. Montblanc's mind, once a sharpened steel dagger, was to give way irrefutably to rust, his body to a similar fate. And what is this going to mean for his future plans? How does the prodigal problem solver approach this? I don't know. I don't know what he's thinking. I don't know anything. I'm not a detective.

But what if I were?

★★★

The year is 2022. Maxime Montblanc has retired from the worlds of business and politics and now, after finding a new vigor and determination within himself, works as the nation's most cunning and effectual private detective. And at his side? His most trusted friend and partner—me. Yessir, we've been all over this great land from the forests of Tofino to the beaches of Prince Edward Island. We've played chess under the Northern Lights in Whitehorse and waded across the shrill waters of the Saint Lawrence. Always in pursuit of a case, always in pursuit of justice. But this new case? Well, it brought Max back to a place he knew all too well, back to a place he swore he'd never go back to again.

Turns out a Member of Parliament had just been murdered. Quite the grisly case as I understand. It had happened sometime that morning. Neither the local authorities nor the press had been informed. The folks at Parliament Hill were hoping that Max could work some of his magic and solve the case before making it public and inviting widespread pandemonium. We arrived on the Hill an hour before noon and were hastily taken to the scene of the crime—the kitchen of the Parliamentary Dining Room.

A grisly case indeed. The naked body of Liberal MP Michel Renault had been stung up by the wrists in a Jesus Christ post hanging now one foot above the stainless-steel food prep counter. Renault's body had been opened in several areas: the inside of each thigh, each forearm, the neck, and the biggest cut from his sternum to his navel. The killer had left a collection of pots, bowls, and glassware directly underneath the hanging body and the blood, most of which had been emptied, was almost entirely contained within these receptacles save for a few splashes that had crusted atop the stainless-steel. Directly underneath the body was a white card positioned between the two dangling legs as if were a descriptive plaque for a museum exhibit. The card was blank and featureless save for the words, *le traître,* which had been written in thick black ink from a heavy hand.

"Gosh guh-guh-guh-golly, Mmmax!"

"Gosh golly indeed, my friend. 'Tis a grim affair to be sure."

"What do you suppose it muh-muh-mmmeans?"

"I must confess I haven't a clear inclination at the moment."

But Max's bemusement didn't worry me. Our cases often started this way but I knew that before the day was through Max will have found his perpetrator and we would be off on a new adventure. After taking some more notes at the crime scene, Max decided to question some of the MPs who had been in the building when the crime was thought to have taken place. We first came across Mark Crowe, an old colleague of Max's, who was in the process of carrying boxes full of papers and books from his office.

"Welcome back, Max. Didn't think I'd ever see you in here again. Wish it were under happier circumstances."

"Hello, old friend. Haven't you an intern that could be moving those boxes for you?"

"Ah, I let him have the day off today, he wanted to go camping or some shit. Besides, I don't mind doing it myself. Beats doing actual work, right?"

"We nuh–nuh–need t–t–t–t–to ask you suh–some—"

"Lawrence, please. We need to ask you some questions, Mark. Michel Renault—do you know of anyone who would have reason to think of him as a traitor?"

"Besides pretty much everyone in Quebec you mean? Look, people around here liked Michel, myself included, but he had lost pretty much all of his favour in Quebec. Look at his voting record. He's a francophone that voted to limit Quebec autonomy whenever he could. You know how that works. Half the province probably sees the guy as a traitor, especially the people that voted for him. Truth be told, he was a nice guy but kind of a shitty politician in that regard. Didn't really do much to keep the favour of his constituents. I don't mean to tell you how to do your job, Max, but if I were you I'd start looking into Quebecers that have a known history of extremist separatist activity."

★★★

(This is about where the commercial break would be.)

★★★

When we come back, Max and I are talking to Grace Aitken, the assistant to the Parliamentary Librarian of Canada and one of Max's 'closest' associates during his time as an MP.

"How's your wife, Max?"

"Thank you for asking. Listen, Grace, I was hoping you might use your RCMP connections to pull a little information for me."

"Of course, whatever you need to help find this guy, just let me know."

"I need you to pull all criminal records from Quebec of individuals with separatist affiliations, specifically those who lived within Renault's riding."

"Sure thing, Max, I'll give you a call as soon as it comes in. Think you might have this case wrapped up in time for a drink tonight?"

"I think with an incentive like that it won't be a problem at all."

★★★

It's getting late in the afternoon now. Mr. Seabrook, the head of security at Parliament Hill has given us until the end of the business day to solve this crime before he brings in the official authorities. Max and I have questioned several people but we don't seem to be any closer to finding a perpetrator. Joined by Mr. Seabrook, we decide to search Renault's office for clues. The office is scattered, papers and books cover much of the floor. Max picks up on the disorder immediately.

"I've always known Renault to be an orderly and organized man. Tell me, Seabrook, why is his office in such uncharacteristic disarray?"

"He had only just moved into this office yesterday. Looks like he was still in the process of unpacking everything. Damn shame that he never got a chance to enjoy this office though, it's got one of the better views in the whole building."

"Quite majestic indeed."

"Look, I've given you all the time that I can give ya. I appreciate you trying and all, but I'm afraid I gotta call this one in now."

At that moment Max's phone rings.

"Max, it's Grace. I've got a list of names for you, and get this, one of them boarded a plane to Ottawa last night. We ran his credit card, he's staying at a hotel across town."

Max thanks Grace, hangs up his phone, and leads us out of Renault's office. As we rush down the hallway, we once again run into Mark Crowe, still in the process of moving boxes out of his office. Max stops and Mark addresses him.

"Hey Maxy! You're moving pretty fast, you found the guy or what?"

"Indeed we have. Mr. Seabrook, detain this man. Lawrence, call the police."

"Me? Come on, man, don't be crazy. I couldn't have done something like that!"

"You wanted Renault's new office. You both wanted it. It's nearly a half meter longer than this office, it's directly across from the men's room, it has an undisturbed view of the river, it's better than your current office in every conceivable way and you couldn't handle the fact that Renault was going to get it instead of you so you murdered him and attempted to frame a Quebec autonomist."

"But how? How did you figure it out? I was so careful!"

"You were careful, Mark. You made it seem as if it were an act of political extremism. You pinned it on a separatist who you knew was going to be in town. You even made sure that your intern wouldn't be here to witness anything. Indeed, you were careful, but you forgot one crucial thing."

"And what's that?"

"I'm Maxime Montblanc. Take him away, Seabrook."

And roll credits! See you all in next week's adventure when Max and I disrupt an illegal seal-hunting operation off the coast of Nova Scotia.

★★★

But of course, I'm not really a detective and I know that things don't play out like they do on TV. I know that story was ridiculous, poorly written, and riddled with tonal inconsistencies and plot holes. I know that M and I won't be traveling the country solving crimes together in the future. I know that once I'm finished with his book he will send me home and I'll likely never see him again.

I know that I'm not really a detective, but I don't need to be. Right now the truth was plain enough. Max was sick. And I don't think he planned on getting better.

# 57

## PAYNIMRY

THE LIGHTS ON the menorah are pinched out by calloused finger-tips that don't mind the heat of the flames as you or I might. It gets darker and what it becomes in here is obvious—it's a meditation on the very process itself. God is perfect and in us He fills with urine and phobias. There's a corpse on the bottom of the shallow lake still holding a mirror and still separating sediment with fine raven hair. M has a wife and follicles and dead skin of her might have been entering my lungs and suddenly I am intimate with her as our bodies collide and combine. Does M still go down on you? Tell me his routine in so much as it defines the man I am meant to be defining. I don't know her name. Women are all nameless to M. God is perfect and so would have been the feminine were it not for M and his desecrating member flailing wildly and unkempt. He fathered Oshawa. Oshawa is an Ojibwa word that white fuckers have translated as portage, that is, the place where one must carry their canoe. No trick of the court mage that I would end up here with canoe overhead and propped up by my thin buckling arms. Fragility forgoes forceps. The slapping sound of M's pelvis against her buttocks rhythmic and controlled as a performing percussionist. We have it under microscope. He has it under lock and key. I recite the poetry of greater men and women—closer to God's perfection—I stumble over words and get them wrong and they walk on me and make me lick their feet and I thank them for the opportunity to do so. His wife invites me inside out of misplaced motherly intuition and she wipes the blood off of my face and skinned knees but she gets too close and I have come to prove my worth. What am I compared to him but she gives notes and encouragement and I almost believe her. I want to see us explode, I want to hear the branches shake and the critters scatter and I want to believe her and I want to believe that this was meant to last forever and that God is perfect and that I embody his perfection and that I am fucking her good but I am not so brazen and I am not so ecclesiastic and I have been waiting for Leonard Cohen to conduct my bris with his personally engraved izmel and I wait here in Oshawa with no canoe to carry and no water to place it in and no knowledge to fashion one because I am devoid of culture and heritage. When we finish I ask her when M will be home and she says she doesn't know but if I wanted to go again there would probably be time enough but she's a little sore and maybe I should use my mouth and so I oblige because I would never dream of talking back to her because she has excellent posture and speaks so well and she's so perfect that I just want to weep. She says I've done the front, now do the back and so I do. And I want a canoe so I might set about the lake at the orange dusk between the reeds and framed within the mountains while ignoring my reflection in the mirror held by the corpse at the bottom. Can we ever walk along the dilapidated train tracks and smell the rust in the air? Can we ever promise that we will run parallel as they do until our own bodies rust and decompose? Can we jaunt at the same speed with hands held through the sun-kissed fields and the fresh fallen snow as we remember fondly the feeling of the other? Can we alternate between the smell of forest soil and our own secreted fluids? Will we always want to? One day they will carve marble statues of us in our various positions and the oblivious masses of the future will gaze upon us as we did ourselves. Oshawa falls to the flood and suddenly no one can find their canoes. We ramble on in all directions but M finds me and he wants to know why his wife smells the way she does and he confronts me and it feels a little too personal for me. I crawl and I crawl back into my damp hole where I can masturbate to the memories I shared with her. Spiders and flies lay their eggs around me and I see that they have done it right. The Canadian identity is slipping away. Canada is having an identity crisis. What could I possibly offer to bolster our culture but for this meditation on the process itself? M will save us, I always suspected that he might though I do not suspect that I will be casting my vote for him. Not after knowing what I know. That's my right and I must cherish it above all things. My heart soars on the sounds of forgotten chords. I could live in hope. Freedom is nothing and it means nothing. Save us from ourselves and come in whatever guise suits your mood. The angry father or the loving mother all end and all end and all end. No one was allowed to cry in our village, it was to be the village of smiles and so it was until the White Men came and claimed our land, our women, our livelihood. And in their conquest they dared to ask what we called the village. We called it Oshawa, and so it is called to this very day. You would know. You would know it all if I told you enough, but I don't want that responsibility anymore. It gets dark in this hole and I can only wait for the servant that God sends—be it M, his wife, or any of the others—to take the blade to me, to drag me from the hole, to carry me over their heads as if I were a canoe, and to throw me into the lake with all possessions stripped save for the flawless mirror bound to my hands.

# 58

## Pariah

Today I finished the final chapter of M's book, a feat which has left me in something of a conflicted state. The book is done, as is the job I was paid to do all summer. While there is still much work that needs to be done in the way of edits, organization, and minor rewrites, those tasks will be sent down the assembly line to other faceless factory workers. I have gifted this body with skeleton and guts and now some other peasant under Montblanc's serfdom will drape it in skin and cloth. A trying writing session this final one was. I had to wrestle quite intensely with the words that floated by and those that the fingers followed through on. What I wanted to write was something resembling the following:

The first light's vicar was born and bred as Maximus Montblanc, his name meaning quite literally 'The Greatest White Mountain' depending on which interpretation you choose to subscribe to. And 'choose' was always the significant word in this regard for no morals spoon-fed or spelled carry with them the weight of their cryptic cousins. In decency of the recent events concerning the new, the unfound, and the relearning, we rest on this, the most silent of meditations. For those who would crack the spines, those who would use the hardcover to smite spiders and mites, and those who would bend the corners of the pages to save your place, there is nothing else you could have done and I applaud you for so elegantly Restoring Conviction. What is Canada to you, M? Canada is a black sail in the sunset and I intend to steer her righteous and true toward the brightest lights of tomorrow. What is righteous to you, M, and how can we seek the light when it remains so beyond our sight? Shut your mouth cretin I, by right of God and Democracy, have no obligation to

provide response to any of your asinine quandaries. And he leaves
on legs like trunks and there was our peace. A man is an island,
or something to that effect, and mine sinks as the sea slowly swal-
lows the sand. Master Montblanc, this man most deserved of
your votes and veneration, from rooms apart reminds me that the
stovetop remains naked and fix it and address it and do something
useful for once in your miserable life. I prayed once to Jah, I once
prayed to Cohen, one's praise now makeshift and swollen. They
make doors the height that they do so that men and women of
normal verticality may pass through them without concern. But
what of history's giants with minds too valuable to be jostled by
the tops of doorframes struck? You read them and you commit
their names to the canon while the rest of us are mulched and
minced into powder for those with additional ends. I had a thing
for ladies in corsets but when she tried one on for me it all
became too real. I wanted to shrivel up and die. Occasionally I
still do. She teaches children now. People ask me what she does
and I say I wouldn't know. But I do know. She teaches children
now. She wears flowing dresses and speaks softly to the children
that she all knows by name. Maybe she still has the corset. Maybe
some of the mommies and daddies fantasize about what it might
look like on her when they meet at the parent-teacher confer-
ences. My words are arranged by vapidity and project my
accomplishments accurately. On a good day my hair is Morrissey.
On an average day it's the cup from that fast-food chain on the
side of the road that you walk by on your way to work in the
morning sea. I miss M when he leaves the room and you will all
miss him soon enough. I, keenly trained to the nuance of cultural
scripts, once thought this was all careening toward some sem-
blance of closure or conclusion. I hinted that it might before, but
now I am confident in affirming it plain. And thus ends the second Greatest Story Ever Told, that of Montblanc's rise to power,
emblematic as it is of our Canadian values. May you read it to
your children at night as their imaginations solidify, may you chip
away at it during your lunchbreaks between bites of refrigerated
couscous, may you display it proudly on your bookshelf between
similar signifiers of sophistication, may you misinterpret the

message of the medium and apply it indiscriminately. To that
which remains pure in this great nation of ours, I bid you goodnight.

That's how I wanted to end his book. How I really ended it
was on some trite and hackneyed note along the lines of:

> *What the great tree that is Canada has provided for me is
> that which I have in turn endeavored to provide for its saplings.
> Mine has been a journey of fortuitousness, perseverance, hard-
> ship, and blessing, and while the road has occasionally provided
> challenge, it is one that I would gladly walk again, for to live
> in and serve this country as I have, and by God's grace will
> continue to do, is a privilege I am eternally thankful for.*

Either way, it's done. I feel weightless and proud and now a
little embarrassed for admitting that I feel weightless and proud.
I hammer the mouse as I click the save icon on the document. I
hammer it three more times. M should be home later this
evening. That's when I'll tell him the good news. But for now,
I think I'll fix myself a drink of something expensive and unpro-
nounceable from Montblanc's stores.

★★★

I hear Max open the door upstairs and I resist the urge to
rush him as he does. I find resolve enough to wait until we are
sitting down for dinner to tell him the good news. I think I'm
beaming. I'm a child about to show his parent the giant 'A'
scrawled across his spelling test. I have been anticipating his reaction all day, the praise he is sure to shower upon me the respect
and admiration I must finally deserve. Ignite systems and go.

"So tuh-tuh-today I finished the b-b-b-book."

"Very good, Lawrence. I suppose we should see about getting you home then."

## 59

## POLEMICISTS

EACH JOURNALIST AND each reporter is a shell in the fusillade launched against the man at the podium. With elegant adroitness M² dances the steps of this rigadoon with his Hydratic partner, even as they attempt to plunge their parazonium into his spine. They, steadfast in their orgulous mission to expose him. He, a modern miracle. And I, a scrivener who always believed that the subtext was more important to history than the words themselves. The following exchanges should be interpreted thusly.

★★★

*Mr. Montblanc! The anarchists! The socialists and the communists! They propagandize and corrupt the minds of our youth! For just last week I caught my beloved son, my darling beautiful boy, fellating a married man.*

There is no place for the state in the bedrooms of the nation. As for the reds, they will be safely quarantined and fettered within the walls of the universities where they cannot reach us. There they may corrode under the weight of their ideals. And Marx my words, friends, they shan't be shown any pity from me. I will stamp them out and they will either lick my boot or suffocate underneath it.

*Mr. Montblanc! You francophone coward! Why must I see your language on the packaging of my foodstuffs? Why can't my daughter get a job with the federal government without sullying herself and learning your dying tongue?*

Your daughter will be given a position in my cabinet. See that she can form a tight seal with her lips. See the heritage of

your family tainted with the blood of the French kings. Thank
me for the opportunity.

*Mr. Montblanc! The children of our nation grow fat and languid!*
*How do you intend to keep our future stock robust enough to carry our*
*legacies on their backs?*

I have the stamina to outrun men half my age. I will be a
model for all, for I do not drink pop, cola, or soda.

*But are those not just three words for the same thing?*

The rule of three you maggot.

*Mr. Montblanc! Our enemies conspire against us! They come from*
*foreign lands speaking languages that fall harsh and strange upon our*
*ears! How do you propose to protect us?*

I will devour the hearts of my enemies. Close the borders
and burn their shops. Next question.

*Mr. Montblanc! How do you cope with the libelous words written*
*about you?*

I protect and cherish the right to produce calumny, even
when directed at myself. But if elected I promise to draw and
quarter anyone who is caught sanctimoniously slinging slander.
Unemployment will drop throughout the land as capable young
workers are hired *en masse* as regional executioners. They are my
appendages, they slice through necks like warm butter. Fear and
love inspires us all. Your books will be burned while mine will
be used for recitation rituals where young cubs may be rightly
indoctrinated into the family. On this I will speak no more.

*Mr. Montblanc! What of your opponents? They have set to captur-*
*ing the impressionable hearts and minds of the nation while you toil*
*unseen in boardrooms and in bordellos. How will you ever catch up?*

My opponents are milksops and knaves. Pitted in combat
against any or all of them I would remain the last man standing
atop their pieces. Hearts and minds, is it? The nation does not
vote on such abstractions. How can they? Their hearts lack
courage and their minds lack any substance at all. They will vote
for me because I am the biggest candidate. I am the most affluent
candidate. The people of this nation are timid are easily fright-
ened. They fear their neighbours, they fear each other, they fear
the future, they fear themselves. I make them feel safe. And such

is the grandest folly of democracy laid bare and my legacy all but guaranteed.

*Mr. Montblanc! Regale us with a tale of your childhood!*

Was that a question or a demand? I am the king, you are the worm, do not think me so prone to your puppetry. My childhood was spent exhuming the bodies of those I've beaten. I walked beaches. The styles have changed but the reactions have not—your wives and your daughters foam and in heat throw themselves at my altar, doing things to me that they have never done to you.

*Mr. Montblanc, how will you cope with the illness that—*

This arrangement is over. Scamper away now, cockroaches.

## 60

## Panacea

Just over two days ago I wrote the last word of M's book and now tomorrow morning I will be flying back home. M booked me a seat on the plane. He paid for it. He even insisted that he drive me to the airport personally in the morning. Buying plane tickets on short notice is something I have never had to do. I doubt I ever will. But M knew how. M knew exactly what to do. He always does. My suitcase is packed. One more night on this cushy guestroom bed and then by this time tomorrow I'll be back on the sunken mattress in the corner of my room. I've spent the last two days making some minor edits on the book. I had to convince M to let me do this. What else was I supposed to do. I have trouble readjusting. I have trouble accepting finality. Don't we all. Spending most of my summer in the proximity of one of the most powerful men in the country has sundered some of my expectations it would seem. I have my understanding of the man. I have written into the world another. They are not in harmony. I don't want this to end because I alone knows what comes next.

The flight is early but I'm having trouble falling asleep. I don't think I want to. What if I had to stay in this bed forever. What if I had to stay in this bed forever, and a French horn section blows the dirge of my dynasty's first dance. What if Montblanc, even after securing the highest of elected offices, still brings my breakfast down to me each day. What if I could stay here and read up on Chinese history and memorize every book in M's study. What if I never had to be seen or heard by anyone but the Lord of the Manor. And what if I could stay here forever in this bed instead of flying west to the unfound life waiting for me in that decrepit hovel I call home. And what if he stayed here forever too in the good health that my presence might provide. What if I didn't have to wipe the dust off my makeshift bookshelf and my dictionaries, my stuttering therapy books, my Bible. What if I didn't have to keep my head down in my hometown for fear that someone connected to it all might see me. What if I could stay in this bed forever, digressed and lessened, yes, but dry, feet turned straight away from too-high diving boards and the tenebrous water beneath. What if—

You know what? I just hope they serve breakfast on the plane. Some coffee at the very least would be nice. Black as it comes if you would.

## 61

## PROTANOPIA

M, CERTAIN COURTESIES internalized, opens the trunk of his car and places my suitcase inside for me. He takes his seat behind the wheel appearing comically oversized as he does. It's an hour's drive to Pearson International wherein I will board a direct flight to Vancouver. And around the same time that I return to the mattress in the corner of my bedroom and the indistinct life that surrounds it, M will officially be beginning his campaign for Prime Minister.

It's early and our drive is mostly quiet. I sneak a glance over at M but I can't tell if he's reflecting on me the way I am on him. I'm hoping for him to deliver some sense of closure, but at this point I know him well enough to realize that it likely won't be coming. I suppose I could ask him how he feels but I can already anticipate his response. 'I've paid you to do a job, Larry, and now that job is done, so let's not dawdle on circumstance.' I'm just another business transaction to the Mighty Montblanc. Another means to an end. Truthfully, it doesn't feel particularly great, but I don't know what else I could have expected. It's not like him and I were going to become best pals. Should I ask him to keep in touch? To drop by for a visit next time he's on the West Coast? He's not going to have time for that. It was only a few days ago I was writing the last words of his memoirs, and now he's driving me out of his life for good. I think I'm justified in feeling a bit used. Well, I suppose the money is meant to account for that.

Dear Lord, the money! Is it bad that I feel much better whenever I remember the money? Max provided me detailed instructions on how to receive my payment. I had originally hoped for a briefcase full of organized bills like you see in the movies, but he reminded me that I wouldn't make it on the plane with that. Then I asked if he would be writing me a cheque. 'No', he says. It would bump me up several tax brackets and I would lose a lot of it that way. Instead he says that one of his 'associates' will arrange to deliver my payment directly to me when I'm back home. If it were anyone else this arrangement would seem pretty damn fishy, but I trust him. After every heinous thing I've learned about the man, I do trust him. You heard it here, people, first thing I'm going to buy is a new damn bed.

★★★

Ten minutes pass with no words between us and just as I am starting to nod off to sleep, M starts speaking, his eyes focused on the road ahead the entire time.

"There is a dream that comes to me frequently now—though I do not believe it to be one of prophecy or veiled warning delivered by some force extraneous or internal. In this dream I am not a grand architect or mainstage player, I am but a silent observer incapable of wandering from the road before me. It is a road that can be seen with open eyes. A road from that place I used to call home, still there and still dusty as it always was. It is an industrial road on the outskirts of town and situated alongside it you will find an oversized carwash meant for cleaning semi-trucks. There is a graveyard of automobiles, their stripped skeletons on display, and next to this a gas station with two seldom used pumps. There is an automobile repair shop. Parallel to this road are the train tracks and an abandoned train station. Mountains painted thick with pine trees block the horizon on either side. There is a storage facility with several orange doors in a row, the doors noticeably brighter and distinct from the dominant dusty grey palette. Chain link fences and wooden powerlines sag slowly toward the ground. There is a faded yellow school bus in one of the many dirt lots with its wheels removed and rust on its underside. This bus has always been there. It still is as far as I know. I have not driven this dusty road in a very long time, and while I can still see it plainly in my mind, in truth I have no idea whether it resembles what I have stored in memory. I suppose that doesn't matter. In this dream I am on that road and none of the surreal or nonsensical logic commonly found in dreams is present. All is as it should be—save but one thing. In the alleyway between two buildings there is a stairway that leads to another building nestled out of sight behind them. This building is not really there. In my dream it is nighttime and I find myself walking on the side of this dusty road. There are no signs of other people around and yet I still feel uneasy, as if I am about to be accosted or assaulted at any moment. I feel a strong desire to run home, yet I continue walking in the opposite direction down this road until I come to the alleyway between these two buildings. And there I see the staircase. It is a metal staircase, inelegant and designed only with the purpose of utility in mind, a staircase you might see in a sawmill or derelict factory. At the top is an inconspicuous door. I ascend the steps, they sway slightly under my weight, and open the door. And inside is the restaurant, its red interior a stark contrast to the grey now me. From the immediate entrance area my vision of the restaurant's interior is limited, blocked by the placement of the dark oak walls. I can see two or three round tables by the windows. They are covered by red tablecloths and have empty wine glasses resting atop them. I can see the corner of the bar, it's solid marble. I hear people inside, but I am unable to see any of them, save for the *maître d'* standing at the podium in front of me. Everything outside feels even more dangerous to me now, but I am at ease inside the restaurant. I am safe. Every night I approach the *maître d'* with the intention of entering and every night he politely, yet firmly, reminds me that I have no reservation and that I will have to leave. At this point I have but a few seconds with which to see as much of the interior as I am able before I am ushered back to the grey night outside. And although this dream follows the same script without variation, every time I am able to see just a little bit more of this restaurant. I see the details of the ornate artistry on the glasses hanging above the bar, the collection of coats hanging in the closet behind the *maître d'*, the red plush of the empty seats. And while I am never able to see anyone else on the inside, I know that just around the corner they are there and they are waiting for me, and I know that I want to be with them. But every night I am instructed outside and once again overcome with the urgent fear of an imminent threat. The dream ends the same way every time—with me running vigorously as I can back to a home that no longer exists."

I don't feel any need to respond to Maxime. I look at him, smile, and let us slip back into silence.

★★★

We've nearly arrived at the airport passenger drop-off area. M reaches into the inner pocket of his jacket, produces a business card, and hands it to me. I examine the card and see that the only things printed on it are a name, Vivian Chan, and a phone number. Before I can ask, M provides the answer.

"That is the phone number of Vivian Chan. She is the head of the Canadian branch of **[REDACTED]** Publishing. As you know, they are the company that will be responsible for publishing and promoting my book once they have finished with the requisite edits. On that card is Vivian's private number. As a personal favour to me, I have let her know to expect a call from you at some point in the future. Understand what that means? She has agreed to personally read anything that you are ready to submit for publication. I cannot guarantee that she will publish anything you choose to send her, but at the very least she will read it herself, which is far more than can be said for most submissions."

Before I can thank him or even process what this possibility really means, we arrive outside the airport. It was as if he had planned to the minute when he was going to tell me this so that we wouldn't need to linger in the potential discomfort of it.

"And here we are."

He parks the car, steps out, and proceeds to lift my suitcase out of the trunk for me. And as we stood there at the passenger drop-off area outside Pearson International Airport, M extended his hand toward mine. I meet his gesture and we shake hands, his powerful grip and large hand engulfing mine.

"*Au revoir*, Lawrence."

Without once looking back he disappears into his black car and drives slowly out of my view.

And that was the last time that I would ever see Maxime Montblanc.

## 62

## PLIABILITY

BELPHEGOR HASN'T A home in this soul nor body. I think about Maximus the Conqueror and his wife that I will never meet. The mimicry and mockery and mirth of the *tabula rasa*—those we wanted to be with shared beds and always uncertain where we would open our eyes. Before unpacking my bags as M's guest, before the mattress in the corner of my bedroom back home, before *Restoring Conviction,* before the pile of rejection letters, before the weight of idealism cast off, there was the idiot kid molested by Belphegor with bright eyes looking only forward toward a future with you.

You were special, but not like I was. Mine was a condition of severed words, not severed thoughts. Yours, they say, kept certain things from processing. And maybe some of me was lost. Maybe some of me never passed through proper. You showed me patience when few others would. Enter late nights of exchanging run-on sentences with carefully selected fonts and colours. Primal fire comes dressed as a muse and paints genesis with light hands. You wrote my name with a capital letter and you used it often. I never had such boldness, opting instead to craft juvenile metaphors under candlelight while the world was sleeping. And I was convinced in those moments that I knew what happiness was supposed to be.

Your father was in the Navy, but now he drove a truck during all hours of the night along quiet and cold backroads— conditions he emulated in his home. I practiced my introduction countless times though I still managed to mangle most my initial words. Your patience, it would seem, was not an inherited trait. My passage was gained under the pretense of mathematical predilection and secured under my offerings of tutelage.

It was around this time that the dream first came to me. It's come innumerable times since and never with any variation. There's a serene lake and it's completely encircled by steep mountains. Both water and sky are clear and calm. And there I am, floating above the lake in a net that's suspended by a panoply of brightly coloured balloons. The net limits my movement, but the balloons keep me floating at a safe distance from the water beneath. Though trapped, I am calm. This calmness lasts a short while before the murder of crows appears from behind the mountains. They fly dense and resemble an oil splotch on the sky. One at a time, the crows approach and begin pecking the balloons above me, immediately popping them with sharp and mangled beaks. The net descends closer to the waiting water with each destroyed balloon and fear fills my heart, but right as I am about to be submerged, I wake up. This happens every time without exception.

Back then I would have this dream almost nightly, but over the years it has become increasingly uncommon. I don't know the reason for this.

All I know is that I miss it so much.

# 63

## PALILALIA

*"GOOD AFTERNOON, PASSENGERS, this is the pre-boarding announcement for Air Canada flight 117 to Vancouver. We are now inviting those passengers requiring special assistance to begin boarding at this time. Regular boarding is scheduled to begin in approximately ten minutes. Thank you."*

I watch the boarding agent from my seat on the gate bench as she makes this announcement. She delivers her lines flawlessly as if she's delivered them a million times before. She probably has. She probably hears those words in her head when she's trying to fall asleep at night. Though what may be now mechanical and meaningless to her was surely a treat for me. It feels like I haven't heard any other voices all summer. And as I sat there waiting for the heavenly voice of the boarding agent to invite me onto the aircraft that would soon carry me westward toward some familiar purgation I started reminiscing on the peregrination that was my summer at *Château Montblanc*. And as I did I couldn't help but think of all those 'P' words that I never could say. And how free those words then flowed as I saw what lived inside!

I saw pugilists painstakingly perfecting punches, pelting pampered poetasters. Poltroons performing pantomime, puerile parodies—particularly prurient perversities par powerful politicians placating panicked putschists. Persephone, prayers piously paid, protecting participating patrons. Parallel palisades preventing; peeping peers, patrolling parades, picketing pricks, parasitical propagators. Pavlov, providing peanutted pabulum, pets proud pointers plus puerile poodles. Penumbral pernoctations perhaps pleasing plangent purveyors, Pollock painting pastiche pointillism, purposeless practitioners planning pastimes, prepping pencils, playing *Pictionary*. Prognostication preparing procrastination. Parallel pistons projecting pained poets presenting parsed poems. Promised peace peeking past peerless peaks.

And how deeply I wanted to stand up and shout. *I am not what you think I am!* I swear I never was. I just want someone to know. But though my beleaguered seams fluctuate I resist the urge to stand up on this bench and shout with jangled words what many would consider to be a long overdue apology. Instead I drift toward halcyon days with water and with family and with imagination. Imagination—the only thing that ever saved me, the only thing I was ever any good at. This meditation on the process being our only evidence one way or the other. I reach into my back pocket and observe once again the business card Montblanc left me as a parting gift. Vivian Chan—Publisher. What might just be my last chance. There may be scintillating fates at work, though I'm sure Max would call them by another name. As I hold the card with both thumbs and both index fingers claiming a corner I remember the seemingly simple question that initiated this odyssey nearly five months ago:

"Do you know who I am?"

The words repeat in my mind as I stare at the font of Vivian's card.

"Do you know who I am?"

I hear his voice clearer with each repetition as if it were my mantra.

"Do you know who I am?"

My focus so committed that I almost fail to register the general boarding announcement for my flight.

I place the card in my back pocket and I board the plane toward a future that seemed at once both harrowing and life-affirming.

## 64

## PLANGENCY

*That woe is me, poor child, for thee*
*And ever mourn and may*
*For thy parting neither say nor sing,*
*"Bye bye, lully, lullay."*

ALL GLORY BE to our Lord Father who would grant us relief and protection from the tempest imminent.

My pneuma has merged with Montblanc's, and lo, a piece of me will be with him when he makes his ascent from this mortal coil to the promised lands above. After the cacophonic medley of the beeping machines and the doctors dictating directions and the priest's soft-spoken viaticum and the collective wallow of the nation and the flatlining finale we find ourselves on a staircase of marble guided by golden handrails. And there was Max. And there was the troubadour, the Greatest White Mountain, the unconscionable sinner, the hope of so many and the ire of all others. The childless and the loveless. The boiled-over water. The man unmeritedly marked. And though toward the end his body trembled and quivered ungraciously, he stood now stoic and calm. He was dressed in a well-fitted white suit, the kind his father never would have worn. He looked ahead and he looked above and beyond the marble steps into the clouds but he never once looked behind. His eyes twinkled and shone and may have leaked had he not been focused on the way ahead. He stood there for some time before taking his first step. His shoes, immaculate and white, landed atop the solid marble with an audible click. And so did his final walk begin. The uninitiated would see a man slowly walking these steps in silence save for the rhythmic sounds of his shining shoes, click, click, click. And soon it was that the clicking of his shoes on the marble steps grew fainter and fainter as he ascended into a place where I could not follow.

But as he did I knew the man's thoughts as if they were my own.

One step for the parents he never had the chance to forgive. One step for the mother and the stories she told him about the cathedrals in Quebec. One step for the father and the malignant blood he passed on. One step for the teachers of the Frontier Apostolate. One step for their curious hands and for the permanent separation of carnality and love that they sculpted. One step for the forests of the Cariboo and the promises he made there. One step for the emptiness he would feel his entire life. One step for the angels he knew were there but would never admit to seeing. One step for the man he let into his heart. One step for their pained and pragmatic vow of separation. One step for the wife he abandoned. One step for the daughter he once promised her. One step for the son he never gave her. One step for the family name that died alongside him. One step for the kindness within him that he desperately wanted to show. One step for the image that meant he never could. One step for each stone thrown from his backyard, resting forever now on the bottom of Lake Ontario. One step for each prayer he whispered into each stone before releasing. One step for the reverence he inspired in some. One step for the contempt he inspired in everyone else. One step for the immense wealth he accumulated during his life. One step for the foundation he created and left every penny for. One step for every child's life he saved because of it. One step for the legacy he left behind. One step for his empty house and for the loneliness he always felt inside it. One step for the choral hymns he listened to late at night when no one else was around to hear. One step for every career he made and every career he ended. One step for the condition he hid for as long as he could. One step for the soft smile he left on his deathbed.

And yes, one step for the stuttering writer who was inadvertently allowed to grow closer to him than nearly all others could.

# 65

## POSTLIMINY

LEONARD COHEN DIED one year ago today. I think maybe none of this exists without him. It's an anniversary that has me feeling like maybe I shouldn't be alone tonight.

And so I'm staring out the window while sitting on the upper deck of the bilevel West Coast Express. It's a one-hour train ride from downtown Vancouver to Port Haney Station in Maple Ridge, and while it's a trip I've taken many times, I still like to gawk out the window as I'm sure most people do. Through a cheap pair of earbuds I'm listening to *Songs of Love and Hate* with the volume set to medium-low, the only way the Godfather of Gloom should be listened to. That's the medium-low volume part, not the cheap earbuds part. I should make it to Grandma's house just after six. I'm not sure what she's making for dinner but I know she'll be making strawberry shortcake for dessert and that alone is worth the trip. A couple years ago she gave me the recipe and I had a go at making it myself. I don't need to tell you that it didn't turn out well at all.

It's been about two months since I've returned home.

In the row in front of me a mother is scrolling on her phone while her young son, both hands rested on the base of the window frame, is asking questions about the mechanics of the train without averting his eyes from the glass portal.

"How does the train stay on the tracks?"

I turn my volume down slightly in anticipation of the mother's response.

"It's magnets and electricity."

I don't think that's correct, but who am I to say otherwise.

The song changes and I wonder how he was able to arrange his words in the way that he did. What a pure artist that man was. Even if I could stand tallest amongst his legions of imposters I wonder if I could ever reach such purity. In the two months since I've returned home to B.C. I still haven't written anything that I believe is worthy of being sent to the publisher that Montblanc put me in touch with. In truth, my life is more or less back to the way it was before I was recruited by M, and that might be the hardest thing to admit. See, people like stories, fictional or not, where the main characters undergo some sort of noticeable change between the beginning and the end. I don't think that has happened here, and it's for that reason that I find myself truly questioning whether or not I belong on this track.

In the back corner of the car I see a well-postured woman reading a book.

Truth be told, I have written very little since returning home. Maybe I'm still burnt out from writing M's painstakingly researched memoirs over the course of one congested summer. Maybe that's just what I tell myself to justify my lack of output. I sincerely believed that with all my immediate and near-future financial needs met, my productivity would surge. Turns out my spending habits have been largely unaffected. You can't readily change your instincts after a lifetime of living frugally I suppose, although I did buy a pretty nice pair of shoes that I'm wearing right now. More expensive than any pair of shoes I've ever had, but every man needs a nice pair of shoes. At least that's what I told myself as I bought them.

Maybe it's time to call it in. Hang up the skates, take a walk in the snow and start punching the clock like everyone else. I shift my focus to the woman in the corner and this is where I'll ask you to really stretch your suspension of disbelief, because the book that she's reading? It's the memoirs of Maxime Montblanc.

Now we can start counting the various reasons why this shouldn't be happening. For starters, why does she have access to a book that hasn't been publicly released yet? While I finished the book two months ago, it wasn't due to be released for another couple of weeks yet. I know this because I've been counting down the days with obsessive anticipation. But beyond that, what are the chances that this woman just happens to be reading that exact book, on this exact train, at this exact time, on this exact day when I just happened to be heading out to my grandmother's house on a whim because the anniversary of Leonard Cohen's death had me feeling down? Blame chaos theory. Blame providence. Blame *deus ex machina*. I don't think it really matters, because it happened.

Without thought of consequence I remove my earbuds, stand up, and make my way over to the alluring siren of serendipity. I sit in the empty seat in front of her and do something I never thought I would ever have the constitution to do—I start a conversation with a complete stranger.

"Hey, sorry to bother you but can I ask you about that book you're reading?"

"Oh, yeah, sure. It's an autobiography of a politician."

"Oh, neat. Which one?"

"Max Montblanc. You know him?"

"Yeah, that's the guy that's gonna be running for PM, right? I didn't know he wrote a book."

"Right. Well, it actually hasn't been released yet. I have an advance copy for work."

"Cool, what do you do?"

"I write for the *Herald*. I'm supposed to have a review of it ready to go before the actual release."

"Oh, the Herald! Very cool. So, is it any good or what? Any first impressions?"

"Well . . . can you keep a secret?"

"Sure I can."

"Okay, well, it's going to get a really bad review from me."

"Oh . . . It's pretty bad, is it?"

"Well it's actually really well-written, which is kind of surprising."

"So why a bad review then?"

"Because Montblanc is evil. He's bad for this country. It's not a coincidence that this book is getting released right before a federal election campaign starts. He's probably hoping that this book is going to be good publicity for him, but I'm not going to give him any help."

"Ohhh."

"I'm sorry, I didn't mean to get all political on you there."

"No, that's okay. So, you've probably read and reviewed a tonne of books, huh?"

"Quite a few, yeah. They got me on a pretty rigorous schedule there but I enjoy it."

"So can I ask for your honest, professional opinion on something?"

"Yeah, okay."

"It's about an idea I had for a book. But for real, you have to tell me what you really think, don't pull any punches."

"Okay, hit me with it."

"Alright . . . So, what would you think about a book where a man is recruited to ghostwrite the memoirs of another man, like a famous and powerful man."

"Is that it?"

"That's it. The whole book is just about the one guy writing the book for the other guy."

"Sounds pretty awful to be honest."

"Yeah, you're probably right. Nobody would ever want to read something like that."